FOR PURE LOVE AND HONOR:

BESA PO

THE STORY OF THE
LEGENDARY WARRIOR QUEEN!

HANA NOKA

CREDITS:

Editing:

BRAD M. BUCKLEY

Cover design:

LUAN TASHI

Consultants:

PROF. DR. SKENDER RIZAJ

LE ROI BEAR

To all the strong and unstoppable women out there.

THE KINGDOM OF ILLYRIA
(APPROX. 231 BC - 227 BC)

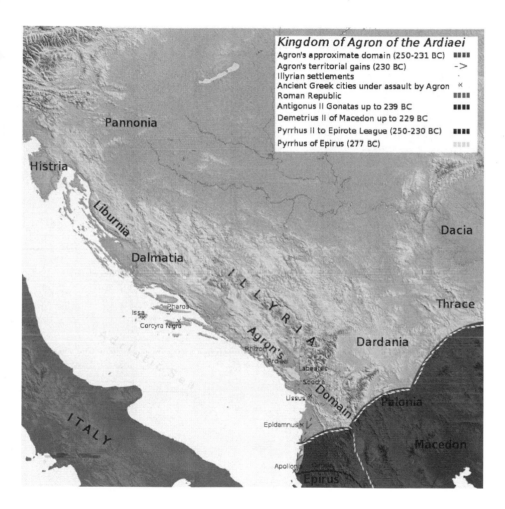

Kingdom of Agron of the Ardiaei
Agron's approximate domain (250-231 BC)
Agron's territorial gains (230 BC)
Illyrian settlements
Ancient Greek cities under assault by Agron
Roman Republic
Antigonus II Gonatas up to 239 BC
Demetrius II of Macedon up to 229 BC
Pyrrhus II to Epirote League (250-230 BC)
Pyrrhus of Epirus (277 BC)

TABLE OF CONTENTS

CHAPTER ONE

THE MIGHTY KING AGRON OF ILLYRIA

THE CASTLE OF ILLYRIA stood at the highest point in the capital of Epidamnus, looking out over landscapes so beautiful that anyone who saw them had their breath taken away. Today, a spectacular sunrise was just starting to peek out from the horizon.

Norik, a short, stout man with jet-black hair and well-trimmed salt-and-pepper beard, entered the majestic round sleeping chamber of King Agron.

"A beautiful morning, my King," Norik announced, thrusting the thick silk curtains aside that kept the room inky black even in midday. He stopped and gazed for a moment at the stunning 360-degree view of the city and surrounding landscapes.

"It's Monday, my King, a spectacular spring day for riding through your beautiful land with your elite soldiers!"

The King pulled the covers over his head to block out the light and groaned.

"Who was it that suggested taking a ride with my guards on Monday mornings?"

"It was you, my King," Norik replied.

"I should have me thrown in the stockade for such an idea."

Norik chuckled, "Yes, my Lord."

"Alright then, since you have deemed to awaken me...."

The King rose up, threw off his covers, and bounded out of bed. He stretched his large, unclothed muscular body, as magnificent as a classic statue come to life. His long, curly blond hair reached his shoulders, framing a handsome face with piercing green eyes. At thirty-five, the King was at his peak physical condition and desired by women near and far. Yet his recent relationships troubled him, and his dreams were mystifying.

Agron led a privileged and comfortable life as prince to the Illyrian Kingdom. Another child would have become callous and mean, but Agron, from a young age, preferred the company of the commoners to that of the royals. By the time he became an adult, the citizens of Illyria trusted and respected him. Agron's father, Pleuratus II, made sure he raised his son to be a hardworking, loyal leader. He saw to it that Agron learned every function of the Kingdom before coming of age, ensuring that the future King would be humble, knowledgeable, and exactly the leader Illyria required. Agron's father had entrusted Norik to teach Agron the ways of women, but his lessons tended to be largely from the male perspective, leaving out vital information that Agron could have used in his struggle to understand the female gender.

Since Norik was a child, sweeping the courtyards and cleaning stables, he had worked hard to rise through the ranks to become a friend and senior advisor to the royal family. Along the way, his tutelage of Agron, especially after the death of Pleuratus II, led Agron to become a wise leader, a humble servant, a trustworthy ally, and a firm decision maker.

Agron's restlessness this particular morning encouraged Norik to hurry the kitchen staff in bringing the King's breakfast to his quarters. Meanwhile, he tried distracting Agron with conversation and drink, pouring wine into an exquisitely crafted silver cup for him.

Agron glanced despondently at the cup. "Norik? What good is all this beauty, all these fine things when love is the only engine of the soul?"

Norik knew his King was in one of his sour moods and was hoping the smell of food would settle him. The last few months had been different in that the King, who was usually full of life and energy, had fallen into a melancholy. It was Norik's job to keep Agron focused, to make sure that, for the sake of all Illyria, the King was happy, for a happy King was a good King. But it wasn't always easy, especially the King and the Queen's separation. It was causing the King to have dark moods that Norik struggled to deal with.

Queen Apollonia was bred to be royalty, just as Agron had been. She was beautiful, graceful, elegant, and poised, yet her arranged marriage to the King had seemed doomed to fail from the start. They had made the best of it at the beginning, attending all events and displaying affection and love, but everything was not as they had tried to make it appear. They had what one might call irrec-oncilable differences.

While Agron desired his nights among the people, Apollo-nia would hardly leave the castle. They had shared much together, including the creation of a son, Rron, and had learned to respect each other, but there was no love between them. It finally became too much for Agron, who was a romantic and yearned for some-thing more.

Since their separation, the King had become prone to philoso-phizing about love. He also was having vivid dreams of a woman so beautiful, his eyes hurt to look at her. She was dressed like a pirate, with long dark hair, shining with sea spray, wielding a sword. This woman seemed to have a fire in her that equaled his own.

"I saw her again last night, Norik," Agron said while consum-ing his breakfast.

"A prophecy, my Lord."

The food seemed to brighten Agron, renewing his energy. Or perhaps it was the memory of the dream.

"Norik! Enough of this restless soul of mine. Today is the day! By the Gods' blessings, today is the day I begin my search to find my true Love! I will be guided to my one and only Queen! Prepare my horses!"

"Yes, my King." Norik had heard his King's proclamation many times, and many times the days had passed with no result. Yet it was his duty to obey, so off he went to make preparations for the quest.

D RESSED IN LEATHER ATTIRE and placing his famous
jeweled sword within its scabbard, King Agron stopped to look at
himself in the large mirror. As a form of self-motivation, he talked
to himself every morning since his separation from Apollonia. It
helped him stir up his energy and focus on running his Kingdom for
the rest of the day.

"Today!" he said to his reflection "Yes! Today! I will be guided
to my Queen! To the Queen of Illyria. I need her, Illyria needs her,
mankind needs her, and history needs her. Love is the only engine
of the soul. So today my soul will feel this power, the power of love.
The power of fulfillment. The power of teaching the world the truth
of love!" The King took one last look in the mirror and stepped onto
the 101 steps surrounding his castle.

As Agron descended, he appreciated the beauty of the gardens,
architecture, and statues of Illyria's greatest heroes standing on each
side of the steps. Amazingly, the castle (completed when King Agron
was just five years old) had never fallen in any of the great wars. Battle
after battle, it had withstood assault from war machines and hordes
of invaders. There were three monstrous walls, each one surrounding the other three hundred meters apart, and within each wall, its
own unique attractions, courtyards, training facilities, and gardens.
Agron knew every inch of them, spending countless hours walking
and sparring on the battlements.

"Your horse is ready, my King!"

Norik was waiting at the inner part of the first gate with White
Dream, the King's famous white horse, and his elite guards. The
gate—twenty-two meters long—was made out of the most beautiful
wood and steel and surrounded by thirty-meter-high walls. Guards
patrolled the walls day and night.

Norik was eager to see Agron in high spirits for the sake of the Kingdom. "Today the port of Pharos has opened all its splendors for you, my King," he announced. "I am sure that with the vast number of people entering your Kingdom through the port you will find the One you seek."

"Well done, Norik!" The King mounted his horse and set off in the direction of Pharos with his squadron of elite cavalry close behind.

Norik watched them until the dust settled and they disappeared over the horizon. He sighed; it was true that he loved the King more than any man, yet sometimes it took much of his energy to keep abreast of his duties. He turned to head back to his chambers for a breather when Arion, the captain of Agron's fleet, appeared at his side.

"Good day to you, Norik." Arion smiled while Norik grimaced.

Well-built with short black hair and large hazel eyes, Arion was feared by Illyria's enemies as well as some of its citizens because of his notorious temper. He had sailed all over the Balkan Peninsula—from Greece to Italy—and had just returned to Epidamnus from his latest campaign the previous night.

Arion and the King had grown up together. They'd been mere boys fighting with sticks in the mud as they watched generals and armies march out of the castle to do battle and return to victorious fanfare and cheering crowds. They both knew their futures would be full of such conflicts so had become competitive over the years, both on training fields and in the pursuit of women. While never revealing his true feelings, Arion was forced to concede Apollonia to Agron, even though he was deeply in love with her. After the birth of Rron, Arion had taken every opportunity to be by the boy's side, assuming the father role that Agron often left vacant while he was off tending to the duties of being King.

Arion was a trusted ally of the King, but he had established an almost obsessive need for the latest news about Agron's family. Norik found him annoying and sometimes neglected to hide his frustration. Arion, however, was clueless; his obsessive focus on news about Queen Apollonia demanded all his attention.

Norik was going about his duties when Arion approached asking, "What is our King's mission today?"

Norik tried to smile. "My dear Arion, what a surprise. This is only the first time you have inquired about the King today. Agron is off to find his true love, his one true Queen!"

"Oh, I did not know that our King needed a new Queen!" Arion responded coyly.

"Yes…well the Gods appeared to King Agron in a dream two nights ago with the good news that he would find his one true love this year," Norik replied. "He was just waiting for a sign in the dream to know the time when this vision would come true, and it seems that today is that day."

Arion grew serious for a moment. "The Gods never lie; dreams are their gift to prepare us for our next journey in life." Then he lightened his mood, "It seems this will be another great day then!"

"May the Gods hear your words." Norik turned to go just as the wild screaming of a child broke through the morning calm.

Rron, the King's thirteen-year-old son, scrambled up to Arion, crying and out of breath.

He threw himself at the captain, clinging to him. "Please, please help me, Arion!"

"What's wrong, child?"

"My mother chased me away; she said she didn't want to see me again today! But I've done nothing wrong." The words were tumbling out so fast the boy could barely catch his breath.

Arion took Rron by the shoulders. "Tell me, what happened?"

"I was helping Dorotea and kissed her on the cheek, nothing else."

Arion smiled and wiped Rron's tears.

"Let's walk together." They started down the path.

"You are thirteen years old now, right?"

Rron nodded.

"You can even get married if you want, because you are a man now, but remember men never cry, not even when facing death. Don't ever forget this, Rron…men never cry! Tears are given to us by a female angel, not by the Gods."

"Nobody has ever told me this, not even my father…Nobody!" Rron looked up admiringly at Arion.

"Mothers teach you how to behave, fathers teach you how to fight," Arion clarified. "Now let's go and talk to your mother." Arion bent over to look Rron in the eyes and make sure he was feeling better.

As they approached the residence of the Queen, Rron hesitated, remembering what his mother had said about not wanting to see him the rest of the day.

The Queen was working in the garden, a large brimmed hat covering her mahogany hair. Her features, even from a distance, were striking—soft neckline sloping up to a smooth sun-stained cheek and stunning face. She turned as Arion and Rron approached, her dark brown eyes first falling on Arion then squinting into a frown at Rron.

Arion watched Apollonia gathering white roses for the day's decorations. "Good morning, Queen Apollonia." He made a mental note of the Queen's flower preference.

"Good morning, Arion. Has Rron been bothering you this early in the day?" She let the fragrance of the roses and Arion's presence brighten her mood.

"It seems, my Majesty, that something went wrong between you and Rron today." Arion made the customary bow but kept his eyes on her face.

Apollonia's guard went up. "It is a family matter; you need not be concerned."

"Yes, but he is our future King, our Prince. He is at an age where he needs to be treated not like a boy but like a man."

"So, if he is a man," the Queen countered, "why did he go running to you to resolve his problem?" She began walking toward the terrace.

"He is confused about adulthood, as we all were at his age."

"Speak for yourself, Arion. At his age, I was already married and well versed in womanhood. While it is true that Rron could find a wife...." Apollonia stopped mid-sentence and turned abruptly to Arion.

"Dorotea is my servant's daughter. It is foolish to think that they love each other. Theirs would be a romance fraught with misery."

"You, more than anyone, O Queen, know what it's like to marry someone you don't love. Do you want the same for your son?"

Arion knew he was overstepping his bounds, caught up in his own feelings toward the Queen. He wanted so to touch her, hug her, kiss her passionately, admit his love for her.

"How dare you say such a thing to me! Get out!" Her wrath was potent, and Arion immediately regretted his comment.

She continued, as if wanting him to both stay and leave at the same time.

"What do you know about love? You and your ships, your men, spending months at sea and in foreign lands. What would you know about love and marriage?" She waved her hand dismissively.

Arion didn't hesitate. "Love is a divine gift from the Gods; it is only their love we should seek. They remind us that our love for other humans mostly brings us pain because we do not understand it. A love that is not pure cannot be understood." Arion was sincere in his philosophy, but the Queen's gaze turned icy.

"Nice words from one who has never been in love."

Arion flushed. "I must go."

"Now so eager to leave? Rron, come here, sit close to your mother and talk about your heart." Rron hadn't been paying attention and had no idea what his mother meant. He stared at his mother blankly.

While pointing to Rron, Queen Apollonia admonished Arion. "There, see that look? That look is the closest you men have to a look of love." Her lips curled with disdain.

"My lady...." Distraught that the Queen could not see how he felt about her, Arion burst out, "My love for you is purer than that of the Gods!" The words tumbled out unbidden and lay there, naked, in the space between them.

Apollonia stood speechless, staring, eyes blinking.

"Rron, go to your room." Grabbing her son's hand, she yanked him up and out the door, all the while staring at Arion.

KING AGRON AND HIS men arrived on Pharos, a beautiful and strategic island that had been lost to Illyria for some time until Agron had reconquered it along with the Dalmatians a few years before. With a large, fertile coastal plain and fresh water springs, it was almost paradise for the Illyrians. A place where the winters were mild and summers warm with plenty of sunshine.

The King paused to breathe in the rich scent of pine forests, vineyards, olive groves, fruit orchards, and lavender fields. The Adriatic Sea surrounding Pharos was as blue as the sky, and its salt air mingled with the other scents to bring back memories of his father. As a boy, he'd listened to his father impressing upon him the need for Pharos to be reconquered for the sake of his people. "The most beautiful island your eyes have ever seen...," his father would say, and young Agron would daydream about the island paradise in his idle hours.

Agron had succeeded in fulfilling his father's directives. Not long into his kingship, he'd conquered the island, and then understood his father's vision; the island was beyond beautiful. In fact, Agron had the sense that the Gods themselves enjoyed the land. After recapturing the island, Agron had directed his commander, Demetrius, to make Pharos the most important port in all of Illyria. Situated across from the Roman Empire, within reach of all the

Kingdom of Illyria, it was the jewel that shone in Agron's long list of accomplishments as a ruler and conqueror.

Agron's trip to Pharos, besides being a quest for his beloved, was also to confer with Demetrius, a man of considerable courage and skill who was known as an accomplished strategist throughout Illyria and Rome. Born to the island, Demetrius was a logical pick to rule it. He was a strong, wise, and often mysterious leader whose heart was hard to fathom and whose loyalties, while never straying from a dedication to Illyria, could be adjusted by the times and situations. Together, he and Agron had successfully fought many battles and their friendship was legendary.

Before Agron made it halfway up the steps to the white stone and rich mahogany residence, Demetrius himself ambled down to embrace the King. Taller than Agron by half a hand and built like a natural warrior, he wore scars on his face and body from years of war. His voice bellowed and his black eyes smiled.

"Welcome back to Pharos, my King!" Demetrius enfolded Agron in his large muscular arms without the formality that was befitting the greeting of the King. The two talked and laughed, walking together until they entered the garden where fruits, nuts, and wine were waiting.

Demetrius handed Agron a goblet of wine. "The port is alive and open with all its splendor today, for the visit of the King. By Gods, it is good to see you!" And they toasted to their friendship.

"How is everything in the capital?" Demetrius inquired. "I hear rumors that Rron is growing and becoming a man."

"True, but still not old enough to rule." Agron moved uneasily past Demetrius, deliberating how to approach the next topic. "I am sure the news of my separation from Apollonia has also reached you."

"It is not my place to mention such personal accounts," Demetrius mused. "I know there was never true love between you. But a friendship still lingers?"

Agron grew silent for a moment. "We must think of the Kingdom and of Rron."

"Of course, of course."

Agron knew that Demetrius was fond of Apollonia and was sure he still had feelings that he kept well hidden. He changed the subject.

"I have heard of the great work you have done here, my friend, so I came to see for myself. So far I have been impressed."

"You flatter me. It is my duty and honor to show you all of Pharos. Yet I understand that I may not be the sole reason for your visit," he grinned.

"You are right. I have had a dream. The Gods revealed to me that my one true Queen and lifelong love would be found in the land that my father wished upon me once it had been restored to its glory. You, Demetrius, have restored the land, and now I must search for my beloved." Agron downed the last of his wine and headed for his horse.

Shocked by the news, Demetrius fell silent. Searching for words, he quickly regained his composure. "Give me a moment and I will get my horse. I am intrigued to find out more about your dream."

The two men rode side by side, with a few of their guards following at a respectable distance so they couldn't overhear the conversation ahead. Demetrius had never seen Agron so animated and excited before. He knew that something important was about to happen, something that could very well change the course of their lives, maybe even the Kingdom itself.

Agron spoke with intensity, describing his dreams in detail.

"I heard a man's voice, a deep and strong voice I can only describe as that of a God. The voice said, 'In a land surrounded by blue water, we have chosen a beautiful woman, strong and intelligent, to help fulfill a great purpose. Her beauty will be like no human eye has ever beheld before. Her strength that of a man, unlike any woman has possessed until now. Her wisdom above any who has walked the earth.'"

Demetrius listened intently, inviting even more detail. The island was limited in size and population, and it would have been hard for him not to have heard of such a woman.

"Patience, my friend," Agron chided. "She may have arrived by sea and not be native to this land. Besides, the Gods have told me more. She will have been raised by her father who was instructed to feed her only wolf milk. She will have fought in many wars and mastered both the art of arrows and sword. Empires will know and fear her. The Gods told me I must find and marry her." Agron drew up his horse and leaned close to his friend.

"That was the first dream. Two nights ago, the same voice came to me and told me I had no time to lose, that they would lead me to her. All I had to do was to ride across the blue waters to a shining island. I am here, Demetrius. I can feel her in my heart; she is not far."

Demetrius was never one to reject a message from the Gods.

"It sounds like we don't have time to waste. This may be an island, but it will take five days to cross end to end."

Beautiful women filled the island of Pharos, more so than anywhere else in the Kingdom of Illyria, and most had been trained as warriors in their youth. Finding the one the Gods had promised would not be easy. Going from household to household, paying their respects at each as custom dictated, was a cumbersome task. Before long, word of the King's search spread throughout the island and everywhere they went, villagers and townspeople gathered, thrusting their offspring into Agron's view in hopes he would pick their daughter or ward.

After three days, fatigue set in. Agron, Demetrius, and all their men longed for the comfort of the castle.

"The Gods did not tell me my search would be so long and arduous," King Agron confided to Demetrius, who looked worn and haggard. The night was approaching.

"Demetrius, for the first time in my life I do not know what to do. I was certain the Gods led me here for a reason, and yet I hear no guidance, I feel no fire. These women are beautiful, but my heart is not moved."

"My King, it is getting dark, and my uncle has a small holding close by where we can spend the night. There is enough room for your men to lie in comfort."

Demetrius led them on a narrow mountain path, their bright torches dancing against the sheer incline and the beauty of Pharos spreading out under the moonlight on the opposite side. After an hour of avoiding loosened stones and falling to their deaths, the path opened up to a fertile plain with a farmhouse visible in the distance.

"We've arrived. Wait for a moment, and I will make the introductions." Demetrius dismounted, approached the large wooden house, and pounded on the double doors.

"Uncle Taulant! Uncle Taulant! I have come a long way with esteemed visitors and would request a night's rest."

Out of the dark emerged two well-armed men with raised bows, startling them. Not even the King's elite guard had heard them.

"Who comes to my land at this hour?" A lean, full-bearded man with long, dung-brown hair obscuring his face leaned forward and squinted at them.

"Uncle Taulant? It's me, Demetrius."

Taulant's sigh of relief closed the gap between them. "It's not often we get such visitors. We thought these soldiers were here to attack us."

Demetrius embraced his uncle. The second archer remained in the shadows still ready with the bow. Agron rode up to the two men, but Demetrius did not introduce him.

"Uncle, I ask to stay the night. Our men are tired and hungry from our long journey. We would be grateful for a respite."

As the King approached, the second archer moved forward, preparing to send an arrow into Agron's heart if he came too close. Now in the light of the torch, the archer's face was visible—that of the most beautiful woman the King had ever seen. Coal-black hair in a long, sensuous braid swung across her shoulder in step with her graceful yet commanding stride. Legs of subtle muscle and feet shod in wolf's fur moved slyly, in sync with her huntress dress of equally black leather. Agron's face grew hot. He clutched at his throat unable to take a breath.

Agron's men rushed to his side. Demetrius approached with grave concern. "What is it, my King? Have you been poisoned?"

As Agron struggled to breath, he pointed up at the woman archer. "Who is she?"

All heads turned toward the woman, and all swords stood at the ready.

The woman's eyes pierced the darkness, defiant and steadfast. "And who is it that wants to know? A sickly soldier begging for shelter?"

Turning white, Demetrius rushed to her, aghast. "Please, cousin, you must show respect." She looked at Demetrius brashly but put away her bow.

"She is the one, Demetrius," Agron whispered. "Even in the dim light of the torches I can see she possesses the beauty I am seeking, and with her actions, the spirit that the Gods spoke about."

"This is my cousin, Teuta. She has been raised far from the cities and towns, trained in the arts of war and womanhood." Demetrius tried to bring Teuta over to Agron, but she resisted.

"What am I, a piece of pottery to be handed to a stranger?"

Demetrius turned to face her, his voice low and serious. "That is your King. He has been searching for his true Queen as directed by the Gods. He has been led to you, cousin, and you must not question the Gods or your King."

Fiercely independent, Teuta did not respond well to situations that made her uncomfortable, but she also knew about loyalty. Trained by her father, a retired commander in King Agron's father's elite forces, she understood respect and honor for her superiors.

Putting down her bow, Teuta kneeled before Agron. "I beg the King's pardon; I am your humble servant."

Agron approached Teuta and offered his hand. He stared at her, silent, eyes moist. Somehow, deep inside, she recognized him but didn't know how or why. Had she seen him at court? In a dream?

Taking Agron's hand, she rose, tingling at the warmth of flesh upon flesh.

"I do not have words, my lady." His voice was a mere rasp. "I need water."

A bowl of fresh water appeared in his hands as if by magic. He emptied it in one gulp without taking his eyes off of Teuta.

Taulant took the bowl. "I am a humble servant of the Kingdom, my King, and I knew your father well. What is it that we can do for you?"

As if stricken by thunder from the Gods and cast under a spell, the King continued gazing upon Teuta. "I would like to ask for your daughter's hand and heart. I want to marry her."

"But, my Lord!" Taulant exclaimed. "We are not nobility or royalty. I'm afraid my daughter is below the station required to marry a King."

"Bah…nobility is a title given by man. The title *Queen of Illyria* is given by the Gods."

Agron finally broke his gaze with Teuta. "I remember your service to my father, Taulant, and if it is the title of nobility you deem necessary for your daughter to be worthy of my hand in marriage, then I hereby pronounce you and your family nobility of the highest order."

Overwhelmed, Taulant cried out, "I am but a simple man; I could never feel comfortable among the highborn."

Agron patted him on the back. "The nice thing about being a King is that I can do whatever I want."

Teuta had had many suitors from surrounding kingdoms and countries, all of whom she'd kept at bay, mainly by proving she was more intelligent and a better fighter than they were. But this was different. She sensed deep affection—an unfamiliar feeling for her—rising to the surface. Teuta was not prone to affection with any man, but this was as though she had known Agron forever, as though she had been waiting for him all her life. Maybe the Gods *had* sent him.

"...daughter?" Her father had been speaking while she was lost in thought.

"I'm sorry, father, what were you saying?"

"It is your decision to be wed or not; I will not stand in your way in either case. I have raised you to think for yourself."

Everyone held their breath because such an option is never presented to the chosen bride; it was always assumed that a betrothal question would be followed by a wedding.

Agron, too, seemed nervous. Teuta had taken him completely by surprise. All he had known of marriage was as a duty, never a passion.

But his heart knew otherwise. "You are the fire in my heart. From this moment on, you shall never kneel in front of another man." The words leapt out of his mouth, words he had wanted to say in private that instead had escaped for all to hear.

"Yes, yes, I will marry you!" Her heart raced and Agron's eyes filled with joy. They embraced for what seemed like forever while everyone clapped and celebrated.

"My Queen, my Queen Teuta."

Demetrius, still not fully comprehending the situation, stood stunned. In a daze, he congratulated his King and his cousin.

Agron slapped Demetrius on the back. "It is time we headed back to Epidamnus."

The King turned to his attendants. "Please pack and make ready. We ride in the morning." Then he held Teuta in his loving gaze. "I have woken from a long dream."

CHAPTER TWO

BESA PO: LOVE CONQUERS ALL

WORD TRAVELED FAST TO the city of Epidamnus that the King was bringing home a new bride, a new Queen. The news heartened the citizens of the capital city because the King had been depressed and sullen for far too long. Apollonia, however, did not take the news well. While her relationship with the King was cordial, the pending arrival of a new Queen-to-be threw her off course, challenging both her status and her son's status in the Kingdom; Agron had promised that Rron would always be the heir to the Kingdom, but what if he had a child with this new Queen?

She was muttering under her breath as Arion approached. He noticed she was not in a good humor and hesitated. Hoping to catch her in a better mood later, he started to retreat, but she saw him before he could get away.

"Have you brought me bad news? Why do you shy away?" Her eyebrows dipped low and her eyes narrowed.

"I just wanted to see how you were, my Queen…. I heard the news."

"Everyone has heard the news; it seems to have traveled like lightning from Pharos." She shook her head and paced the room.

"You are still the first Queen; that will never be in doubt. You are the mother of the heir to the throne." He hustled to keep up with her.

Queen Apollonia kept her rapid pace. "What do you know about her? Who is she?"

"All I know is that she is Demetrius's cousin."

"Demetrius?" She stopped in her tracks, shooting Arion a quizzical look. "Demetrius brought him to her?"

"I don't know, my Queen." Arion fidgeted.

"Oh, stop calling me 'my Queen.'" Exasperated, Apollonia dismissed Arion with a wave of her hand. "We are beyond that now. I will have a word with Demetrius when he arrives."

Arion was beginning to take offense at her tone, but he held his tongue.

"I am sure he will want to talk to you as well," Apollonia predicted.

Arion knew that Demetrius had once had his eye on Apollonia and could be a potential rival. He also knew that Demetrius had spent a long time away, and Apollonia's heart had not strayed from Arion.

T HE CITY OF EPIDAMNUS, situated at one of the narrower points of the Adriatic Sea, lay opposite the Roman ports of Barese and Brundisium. Within the city towered King Agron's beautiful round castle, a fortress with impenetrable walls and overflowing gardens that protected the King's loyal subjects. In the rock apertures on each side within the hall loomed large statues of the Gods. The supreme God was Tomor, the father of all Gods and humans and the lover of Bukura, the beautiful Goddess. There were the Goddesses Genusu—representing Mother Earth—and Prende, the Goddess of Love and wife to Perendi, the Thunder God. And of course, there was Ora—spirits whose influence extended throughout one's lifetime.

Children learned at an early age about the Ora. The Ora lived in the mountains, it was said, in caves, near the rivers and streams. All people were assigned an Ora at birth, the color of which determined whether one was courageous and diligent or lazy and cowardly.

Teuta knew this as she and her father walked through the hall. When she was very young, her mother had brought her here to explain the ways of the Gods and spirits, just as her father had shown her the ways of the warrior.

After strolling for a few minutes in silence, Taulant turned to his daughter. "You seem to be happy. That is good, but I am afraid there will be times when you are not. There will be hard times, dangerous times. I have seen great things for you, my daughter. My Ora has told me much, but everything is not set in stone. You must remember, you always have a choice."

Teuta clung to her father's arm. "You have taught me well. I will not shy away from challenges, and I am prepared for my new life."

"Yes, I know you can handle yourself on a battlefield where swords and arrows are at play, but I am not as confident you know the battlefield of love, of treachery and betrayal. You will face all these things, my beautiful Teuta."

She glanced away involuntarily, then spoke, resolution strong in her voice. "Do you know why we are here on earth, Father? I am here to love a man I am connected to, a man who loves family, life, and his Kingdom. I am here to be part of that love as I am part of yours. I love you, Father."

Teuta hugged her father with all her strength. The two remained there for a moment, embracing until Taulant pulled away.

"Don't ever forget, Daughter, that in order to protect love you must do anything. Anything…even kill if necessary."

He took her hands in his. "I will not be here when big decisions must be made. With your title comes much responsibility and many enemies. Be vigilant. You may not know who to trust, but when you find yourself in doubt, close your eyes, talk to your Ora and ask, 'What would love do?' and there you will find your answers."

Men were approaching. Taulant released Teuta's hands as they came near. A man of medium height and familiar features addressed them. "Good day, I am King Agron's brother Scerdilaidas. And you must be Teuta." He looked intensely at her, passing judgment with his eyes, then shifting his gaze to her left. "And you, her father, Taulant. I have heard many stories of you from my own father."

Scerdilaidas bowed slightly. "Follow me. I have been tasked with showing you your quarters."

Scerdilaidas was a quiet man with long black hair and beard, both of which he kept well groomed. Though he shared some of Agron's features—mainly his cheekbones and eyes—he was also uniquely himself.

Scerdilaidas had never desired to rule; he was more interested in intellectual pursuits, strategy, and philosophy, a subject he often taught. Yet he had been appointed commander of the Illyrian army by Agron and was partly responsible for creating the most powerful army the Illyrian empire had ever seen.

Despite his military success, Scerdilaidas felt little satisfaction in it. His passion was in another direction; he was in love with a blue-eyed, handsome young student named Donat. Each day he would look upon Donat and want him more and more, yet he didn't have the courage to tell him. His was a secret so dire that he went out of his way to show his soldiers and his friends that he was like any other Illyrian man.

Teuta had sensed that something was different about Scerdilaidas, but he seemed quite pleasant so she did not pursue the feeling further. She did find it odd, however, that he never mentioned his potential ascension to the throne—since she assumed he was in line for it—nor even seemed very interested in the idea.

Once the group had settled into their quarters, Teuta asked Scerdilaidas if he would stay and share some wine, knowing that his insights about the Kingdom could be valuable. He declined the offer with apologies. His duties as Agron's brother were pressing, he noted, and he must go.

Scerdilaidas sensed that his brother's new Queen viewed him as a valuable source of inside information and that she was also smart enough to know that such information would be needed in her role as Queen. Yet Scerdilaidas had little patience for gossip or political intrigue. He did not possess the information she was looking for, and it would have been awkward for both of them had they stayed to talk together.

Much of the citizenry hailed Agron's return to Epidamnus with a new Queen-to-be as a glorious event, but some felt quite the opposite and did not share in the revelry. Apollonia fell in the latter category. She remained in her quarters and did not welcome Agron home. Apollonia's clear rebuff was no surprise to Agron. Though he felt a responsibility for her anger, a higher power had spoken and he had no doubt about his actions.

RRON ARRIVED WITH ARION by his side and ran to greet his father as if he had been absent for months rather than days.

"Father, it is good to have you home."

"It is good to be here and to see you, but it's only been a few days." Agron embraced his son.

"It seems longer," Rron declared. "Perhaps because my days have been full with Arion teaching me many things."

Agron's eyebrows lifted. "So Arion has been schooling you since his return?"

Hearing resentment in the King's voice, Arion stepped forward. "I have taught him some little things to keep his mind active. Nothing of any great importance."

Rron interrupted, unable to contain his excitement and newfound learnings. "You taught me about how angels, not the Gods, make tears."

Arion knew that Rron's education was up to his father and to intercede in the process was considered disrespectful. He lowered his gaze. "It came up in a conversation, my Lord. That is all." He bowed his head still further, but Agron pretended he would have none of it.

"I am grateful you have been able to give my son attention when I cannot. I will, however, hold you accountable if he learns inappropriate words or to disparage women." He chased his harsh words with a slight smile, and Arion's hunched shoulders straightened involuntarily. Even though he commanded fleets and hundreds of men quite capably, he still felt intimidated by his King.

Rron looked up at his father, his eyes full of respect but also sadness. "I have much I want to show you."

Agron tousled Rron's hair. "And there is much I want to see, but right now I have pressing matters that need my attention. As King, my responsibilities are great. When you are King, you will understand."

Rron's body slumped with the weight of desire he carried for his father's attention.

"I will see you later," Agron assured him. "Right now, go with Arion and continue your training. I am proud of you, my son. Know that I love you."

Arion felt bad for Rron; he knew that not having his father's attention was hard on the boy. At the same time, he rejoiced both that the King trusted him with his only son and that each time he was with Rron meant he had a chance to be near Queen Apollonia. Arion's fondness for the Queen clearly needed to be kept a secret; he must avoid all appearances of impropriety toward her. Unlike the King, who was free to remarry, the Queen must remain unmarried as long as the King lived.

When the King had departed with his men, Arion took Rron to the archery range. He thought it would help the boy get his mind off family matters.

"Should we try new arrows?" Arion asked as they approached the range. "We will see who is a better archer today."

Rron shrugged. "You will beat me, you always do."

"If you practice every day, one day you will beat me."

Arion helped Rron with his archery form. They worked hard, letting loose two quivers of arrows before Rron spoke again. It was apparent he had much on his mind.

"My father has brought a new wife to the castle, and there will be a big wedding. How do I cheer up my mother? Tears have streaked her face for days."

Arion lowered his bow, aware that his plan to distract Rron had failed and that his duty now was to comfort his young charge as best as he could.

"Time is the best healer," Arion replied. "You must let her find her own way. Pain is part of life; today a thunderstorm, tomorrow sunshine. We must remind her that she is loved and that she is not alone."

"Thank you, Arion. I don't know what I would do without you."

"We all have a mission that is the essence of our existence. The Gods don't always make it clear what that mission is, but I know that mine is to protect you, your mother, the King, and Illyria. I will always be here for you."

Arion's heartfelt words drew the boy in. Rron came over and embraced him. The boy's gratitude touched his heart.

As they were still embracing, Norik appeared, surprising them both. He frowned at the show of affection, but his position demanded him to remain stoic.

"Sir, Agron would like to have a word with you."

Arion nodded.

"I will look after the Prince, my Lord."

"Thank you, Norik."

That Agron should be called to the King's chambers so soon after speaking with him was a bit odd. *It must be a subject that could not be discussed in Rron's presence*, he assumed.

The private royal guard showed Arion into the King's quarters. Dishes of wild boar, greens, and wine surrounded Agron at the dinner table.

"Arion, my friend, come join me."

Arion had no desire for food but sharing a glass of wine would be polite, so he took a seat near Agron to hear what he had to say.

"As you are aware, I have found my Queen," Agron could not contain his excitement. "With the help of the Gods, I have found a woman whom I love and will marry three days from today. She will be Queen Teuta of Illyria."

Arion shifted uneasily in his chair.

Agron took in a breath. "I know you are close to Apollonia, Arion. Do not worry, I have no desire to interfere in your friendship with her; I just want her to know that I have deep affection for her. Her sadness is not so much about losing me—we have had our differences—but rather more about losing her status as Queen. I want you to let her know that she has nothing to fear, that she will always have a place in the Kingdom and the castle."

The King's speech caught Arion off guard; it was at once a show of trust and an insight that Arion had been unaware of. He bowed his head in understanding. Agron rose and embraced him. "I am sure that the Queen will take kindly to your words."

Both men drained their wine cups in silence.

"Is there something else, my Lord?" Arion asked.

Agron raised his eyebrows and carefully returned his cup to the table. "There is."

He motioned for the meal and the wine be taken away. Shifting closer to Arion he lowered his voice, his tone becoming serious. "I have word from our friend, the King of Macedonia, that he has a serious problem with the Dardan and Etoil tribes. It could be just days before war breaks out. We need to form an alliance to protect our borders. I have gathered a force of five thousand soldiers who are standing ready for my orders."

The news surprised Arion; he had not heard of the conflict even through his own network of informants.

"You will take your fleet to support the Macedonian ships once the ceremonies of the next few days are complete. I know you are the best man for the mission, and I trust you will enjoy the festivities; you will be updated before you leave."

Before Arion could respond, the King turned away, preoccupied by the countless responsibilities that fell on his shoulders, including, of course, his own marriage.

Alone with his thoughts, Agron opened the thick curtains revealing a stunning view of the sea. The pounding of the waves on the rocks below soothed the cacophony in his mind. One thought, however, kept rising to the surface, refusing to stay submerged— Teuta and her beauty. How could he feel so strongly for someone? Even war and countless responsibilities were nothing compared to his love for her. He ached for her lips; the sun shining off her hair; her deep, intelligent eyes. In spite of exhaustion from his long trip, sleep eluded him. His mind reeled with thoughts of his future; having Teuta by his side was going to be a joy beyond any he had experienced. He walked into the garden where the dew glistened on the greenery in the moonlight, and he smiled the smile of a satisfied man.

The noises below Norik's bedroom startled him. Leaping out of bed, he drew his sword, ready for the most vile intruder, and raced to the garden. There, he found only the King contemplating a pool of water.

"My King," Norik put away his sword. "Is anything wrong?"

"I cannot sleep," Agron sighed heavily. "I wanted to feel the silence of nature and yet there is no longer any silence."

The King's answer puzzled Norik, but this was not the time to question its meaning. "Should I bring you a girl from the virgin chamber?" He knew that Agron had found lying with concubines useful in the past to help him sleep.

Agron spun almost violently toward Norik, daggers shooting from his eyes. "From this moment forward, no other woman's hand will touch me, no other breath on my neck or body in my bed other than Teuta's. Do you hear me, Norik? No other."

"Yes, my Lord." Norik backed away in shock, the King's words were a harsh slap to his face. "Forgive me, my King, if I have offended you." This King raging in front of him was not the same King who had left on a journey only five days earlier.

"I waited all my life to find her, and now she will be the only woman to ever cross my chamber door. I want you to release all the concubines in the morning. Find husbands for them; let them move on with their lives."

"As you wish, my King." For the first time in Norik's long term of service for the King, fear and anger rose high. This woman had changed the King, and nothing would be the same. Who knew what more she would do to the empire!

Teuta woke up with a start, sweaty from a dream of King Agron gripping her hand as they battled strange, faceless men. Beings of white had appeared suddenly, shining light upon them. The beings sang, and everything around them stilled. Then without a word, they took Agron from her and raised him into the sky.

Teuta's father had taught her to be strong, to fight like no man had ever fought. He had also taught her to be fearless. Yet her dream just now had made her fearful. Her mother, having died while delivering her, was not around to teach her gentleness or love. So the feelings rising up in her were strange, alien. She did not want her first morning in her new home to be full of tears, yet the dream persisted.

A soft knock on the door broke through the web of her thoughts. She wiped her face with her sleeve. "Come in."

The door opened tentatively, and a girl not more than fifteen peeked shyly into the room. "My name is Dora, and I was sent to be of service. If this is too early, I can return." Dora bowed, averting her eyes until Teuta spoke.

"Dear child, there is no need to bow to me or avert your eyes. I am no God."

"Yes, my lady." Dora's eyes still dodged full contact.

"I would appreciate some breakfast and a warm bath."

"At once, your highness."

"Please, Dora, call me Teuta; that is my name. For I am no higher born than you, nor do I have the refinements of a lady."

"Yes...Teuta. I will see to your desires." Dora hurried out of the room.

Teuta was amused and flattered by Dora but concerned that the citizens of Illyria would take her ascension to Queen as a bad omen, an affront to the former Queen, who, she gathered, was popular among the people. Teuta had to put her mind to the wedding and all that needed to be done, but she knew it would be wise to gain the trust and admiration of the citizens. She felt tremendous pressure to perform in a prescribed manner yet did not know what that manner was. Suddenly, Norik appeared at her door requesting that she join the King for breakfast.

Teuta could not refuse. "Tell the King I will be there as soon as I am able."

Transfixed, Norik could not take his eyes from the woman in front of him. He had never seen such beauty. The King's obsession took on new meaning for him—who in their right mind would not find themselves obsessed with such a creature?

"Yes, my lady." Norik bowed and left.

Forty-five minutes passed as Teuta prepared herself to enter Agron's chambers. She requested that Dora send back the breakfast, prepare a bath, and dress her in a simple blue morning dress.

Meanwhile, the King waited anxiously by the door of his chambers, like a pup waiting for his master's return. Finally, a faint swish reached his ears, the sound of fine linen brushing against soft skin.

The King perched on a nearby chair and pretended to be preoccupied. "Ah, my Queen. Good morning." He rose as Teuta smiled, then led her to the sofa. The banquet of food surrounding them included roasted meats, succulent fruit, enticing cakes.

The King pointed to the decadent meal. "What is to your taste?" Teuta's mouth softened. "From today, it is the taste of your lips, my King."

Their eyes met, and Agron was speechless for a moment. He could tell Teuta meant what she had said. Everything seemed part of a whirlwind. Time stretched and contracted. Agron felt he had known this woman for years, yet he knew they had met not more than three sunrises ago. How could such a thing happen? Can love spring so quickly between two people that their lives are changed in an instant? Yet, here was the proof.

"From this day forward, no one but you, my Queen, will know the taste lingering here." Agron pointed to his lips, and as Teuta moved close, he grabbed her long black hair and kissed her as if he had never kissed another. Teuta was not experienced or accomplished in such things, having spent her life being groomed for battle. For her, the force and yet the tenderness was new. Her heart raced and her head swam. How, how could this be? She pulled him closer to her and kissed his neck, ran her fingers in his hair.

"This is the most glorious day of my life," Agron announced.

"There are many such days to come," Teuta replied, her mouth close to his ear.

Lost in the moment, they did not hear the commotion and the abrupt arrival of Arion, who strode into the chambers with a Macedonian messenger and three armed guards. Any intrusion into the King's chambers outside of protocol had to be of great importance. Still, Teuta and Agron glared at the intruders while they covered themselves.

"Please excuse the disturbance, your Excellency. I bring an urgent message from my friend, the King of Macedonia." Arion presented a silver message bottle to Agron.

The King removed the parchment. "Have you read it?"

"Yes, my King, it was addressed to me. I was unaware of the content until I read it, then came directly to you." Arion bowed to acknowledge the truth of the matter.

"Perhaps, then, you can tell me what the letter says so I do not have to strain my eyes." The King was well aware of the situation in Macedonia. He had brought it up to Arion in the first place and was curious why the Macedonian King would reach out to Arion rather than directly to him as king.

"As you wish." Arion cleared his throat, sensing the tension, "Demetrius the second, the King of Macedonia, regrets that he will not be able to attend the wedding. The situation with the Dardan and Etoil tribes has grown increasingly serious. He has lost over one thousand soldiers, and his fleet is unable to protect his borders. He wishes the mighty King Agron a very happy marriage and urges him to consider joining his fight. He assures him a plentitude of gold and plunder to share."

Agron tossed the parchment aside. "Are your ships ready?"

"Yes, my Lord."

"Then it is best you be off. Take two thousand soldiers and support the Macedonian King. I will join you following my wedding."

"My King, there is no need for your involvement. I will have the situation under control." Agron could not tell if Arion was being considerate of his pending marriage or if he wanted the glory of victory.

Sensing the King's wariness, Arion continued. "Any glory of your army is your glory, my Lord. I am a servant to you, the most powerful King in the land."

"Very well, Arion. May the Gods be with you and our army. I will join you as soon as I am able."

"Very well, my Lord. May your marriage be blessed and fruitful."

Arion departed with his entourage. Agron relaxed, falling back on the bed. Teuta had many questions.

Rron arrived at his mother's chambers mulling over his feelings and the situation with the new Queen. He was greatly confused. How should he act at the wedding, for starters? He did not understand how his father could abandon his mother so easily. His sadness seemed all consuming.

As Rron entered, Apollonia motioned for him to sit by her. "I know you are sad, my son. I am sad too. I do not know much about the new Queen, but I am sure she is a fine person if your father has chosen her. As the King, he can marry many times and have many children." Bitterness crept into her voice, but she forced a smile to reassure Rron. "Still, you are his first born and successor. That is important to me."

"Mother, can I ask you something?"

"Anything." She took his hands in hers.

"Did you ever love my father?"

Surprised by the question and more so since Rron was asking it, Apollonia hesitated. It was clear that he had been more aware of the troubles between her and Agron than they had known.

"That is a strange question, Rron. We created you, and that was an act of love."

"But did you love him enough?"

Now she understood. Somewhere her son had heard stories about why she and Agron were no longer together and that if only she had loved the King more, he would not have left her. All lies, but to a vulnerable boy looking for answers....

"Do you want to know the truth? Not the made-up stories of servants and malcontents?" She held Rron's chin and looked into his eyes.

"Yes. I want to know." He said anxiously.

"OK. Ever since I was a child, I have been in love with Arion. We swore to each other that we would be married and have a life together. But then my father gave me away to Agron because we were both from aristocratic families, and it was not possible for me to marry a shepherd's son. I grew to care for Agron. He was good to me, and we had you, which made our bond strong. But did I love him as I have loved Arion? No. I believe that is why Arion remains close to you because you are a part of me." Rron fell silent.

"You must not tell this to your father, ever. Do you hear me?" She grabbed his arms. "This was for your ears only, because you deserve to know the truth."

"I understand. Does Arion still love you?"

"I believe he does, yes. But his responsibilities as commander of the King's fleet are great. Out of respect for your father, he dare not show his feelings for me." She had told a lie, but it was better that Rron didn't know the extent of her ongoing relationship with Arion.

"I think Arion still loves you, just as I still love Dorotea."

If Apollonia hadn't known better, she would have thought her son was manipulating the conversation, but she knew he was merely expressing ideas put into his head by Arion.

"You miss Dorotea?"

"I miss her a lot. I think about her every day."

"I am sorry for taking her away. She and her mother will be fine; I gave them enough gold to keep them comfortable. But you have responsibilities, my son. Your first priorities must be your homeland, your people."

Rron found it difficult to accept such responsibility when he saw those around him enjoy a love that he was denied. Apollonia drew him near and hugged him.

"I love you, my Prince. I will always be here for you."

Rron showed no response, and Apollonia knew that sending Dorotea away would be a sore spot for many years to come.

NORIK WAS OVERWORKED AND running out of patience. The bulk of the wedding arrangements had fallen on his shoulders, adding extra weight to his regular duties. Going to the King for help was not an option because of Agron's preoccupation with the pending war in Macedonia. Guests were arriving from all over the Kingdom, and Agron had instructed Norik to ring the bells each time someone arrived. So between making arrangements and running to ring the bells, he was exhausted.

Then Bersant arrived, tall and thin with white hair and wrinkled face—the wisest of all the counselors and, at sixty-five, the oldest man in the Kingdom. He could not remember a time before he had been in the employ of the royal family, and Agron attributed much of his own success to Bersant's advice. Now it was the statesman's duty to perform the marriage ceremony.

Bersant and Norik had a history together—opposite personalities growing up working for the royal family, the first from an aristocratic family and the second the son of a fisherman—and they often clashed. Their last meeting had ended with Norik storming out after Bersant had insisted the King loved him more. Norik found Bersant to be egotistical, two-faced, and rude, Bersant thought Norik to be weak, subservient, and condescending.

Norik was not in the mood today to deal with Bersant's demands, spoken without so much as a hello. "I need to speak with Agron."

"Of course, he is waiting for you, if you follow me," Norik said through clenched teeth.

"I know my way," Bersant snapped.

"Still, the King has instructed me to introduce all visitors."

"Very well then."

A smile crept over Norik's lips. *Bersant may have the King's ear every now and then*, he thought, *but I have it every day.*

As they entered the King's chamber, Bersant was all smiles and happiness. "It is with a joyful heart that I come today, my King." He

39

bowed and handed Agron a gift wrapped in fine cloth. "For your bride."

"Thank you, what a kind gesture. And indeed it is an honor to have you here. No ceremony would have value without your presence." The King bowed slightly in return, indicating his respect for Bersant.

"I am happy that you listened to me and followed the dream," Bersant commended the King. "I am anxious to meet Teuta."

"She will be ready shortly. I will never forget that it was by your urging I found my heart." He motioned for Bersant to sit. Bersant lowered himself into a chair but leaned forward uneasily.

"There is much to go over with Teuta, oh King, regarding the ceremony, as you know from your previous marriage."

Bersant, while a valued advisor and confidant, was conservative in his views of love and marriage. He issued advice regarding Agron's dreams of finding a new love not so much as a sign of accepting the King's choice to leave Apollonia but more as an acknowledgement of the Gods' hands in Agron's life. Bersant, after all, had been party to the decision, along with Agron's father, for the King to marry Apollonia in the first place. So, it was not easy for him to see the marriage crumble.

Agron nodded to him. "I am grateful for your assistance and encouragement, Master Bersant, and grateful to the Gods for my happiness."

Bersant returned the nod. "May joy, love, and prosperity follow you and your new Queen into the distant future."

As if on cue, Norik stepped out of the shadows to show Bersant to Teuta's chambers.

Teuta sat on the divine by her bed, wringing her hands. She was exhausted. Outfit after outfit had failed to match her desire for wedding attire. Nothing seemed to suit. She had wanted to wear her hunting outfit, because she was comfortable in it, but she knew it would not be acceptable. Reluctantly, she let the idea go. Dora had been patient and accommodating throughout the morning's unintended fashion show but appeared frustrated by the lack of progress.

"My Queen, there must be one dress that would be acceptable to wear for one day; these gowns from across the Kingdom are all beautiful and were made specifically for you." Dora held up a particularly spectacular gown and modeled it for Teuta.

"I know, Dora. I am sorry for being so difficult. This is all new to me.... Fancy clothes make me uncomfortable and self-conscious. Perhaps we can create something ourselves, make our own style." Dora's eyes grew wide with excitement about the prospect.

A soft knock on the door jarred them back to the present. Unprepared for visitors, the two women looked at each other in panic. Dora gathered up the Queen's robe and wrapped her in it as Teuta answered. "Who is it?

Norik's soft voice floated through the keyhole. "It is me, my Lady. I am sorry to disturb you, but I have an honored guest who would like to meet you."

Dora finished securing the robe and nodded silently to Teuta.

"Alright, one moment," Teuta called out. She motioned for Dora to open the door.

Bersant and Norik entered, bowing reverently. "May I introduce you to Master Bersant? He is a respected advisor to King Agron, as he was to his father before him."

"I am honored." Bersant stared at her with the surprise of a teenage boy. He had never seen such beauty. After a moment of awkward silence, he sputtered, "I am a master, a teacher, a friend to royalty, but I have learned a lesson today. The Gods can create divine beauty here on earth."

"I am flattered." Teuta was not sure what to make of the man in front of her, though it was not hard for her to see that this man had the trust of Illyria's elite. He had the bearing of a nobleman and the charm of a politician.

"It is my duty to explain the formalities of the wedding ceremony and to help you prepare," Bersant informed her.

Ah, she thought, *he is by all accounts a teacher, and the visit is a practical one rather than ceremonial.* She relaxed a little and motioned for him to take a seat.

It took well over an hour of Bersant droning on about the specifics of the wedding and Teuta's responsibilities before, at the very end, he noted that the Queen-to-be would be prompted during each step. By the time Bersant left, Teuta was exhausted and needed to nap.

While Dora cleared off the bed, Teuta held up a long, white satin dress. "Fetch me in an hour, and we will see what we can do with this one."

"Yes, my Queen." Dora smiled as she gently closed the chamber doors behind her.

Music echoed throughout the Castle, musicians from every corner of the Kingdom filling the call to play King Agron's favorite instruments—the lute and the lyre. The gardens overflowed with flowers and candles. Aristocrats from throughout Illyria mingled among the splendor of the King's castle, anxious to see the new Queen.

Taulant walked nervously around the colonnade listening to the gossip of women—stories they were telling about his daughter. Wild stories that seemed to be made up on the spot. He finally ended up in the hall of the Gods where he went to pray.

"Gods of Illyria and all lands beyond, please bless my daughter Teuta on this, her wedding day. Bless her with happiness, with long life, and many children." His eyes filled with tears. Then a voice broke through.

"My dear Taulant, I hope those are mostly tears of joy."

Taulant had not been aware of King Agron standing close behind him.

Taulant rose quickly and bowed. "My King."

"It seems we have both come to pray to the Gods. For me, it is to thank them for bringing your daughter into my life. For you, it is another purpose." Agron looked into Taulant's eyes and embraced him. "You should never doubt her happiness. I will always take care of her, always."

"Thank you, my King."

"I have made arrangements for you to remain at the castle; there is no need to return to Pharos." Agron was concerned that his soon-to-be father-in-law was not being taken care of according to his station. Taulant was now much more than a simple farmer and former soldier.

"Thank you for your generosity," Taulant said gratefully. "It seems my job is now done. I hand my one and only daughter to your care. I need to return to my farm and see the plants grow, nurture them as I have done with my child. I will visit from time to time."

T AULANT STOOD WITH TEARS in his eyes before Teuta's chamber. As Dora opened the doors, happiness and sadness mingled to create an unfamiliar emotion in him. And then he saw his beloved daughter in a dress that matched her spectacular beauty. White silk with crimson and gold highlights and pearls—great lengths of them, their creamy color offset by the pure white.

"Father," Teuta beamed as he stepped into the room. "Please don't be sad."

"It is not sadness my daughter; it is pride and joy…. Perhaps a little melancholy for the days past, but now is the way to the future and glory." He kissed her hand and she his forehead.

"It is time, my Queen," Dora announced as she sewed the final touches on the gown. Teuta took a deep breath.

"Shall we go?" Taulant offered his arm.

Teuta took another deep breath that matched the first. "I'm ready."

Arm in arm, father and daughter strolled out through the garden marveling at the light from thousands of candles and the magical glow beneath the flower petals. The music soared. Teuta felt the gaze of hundreds of eyes on her. She was not used to being the center of attention, but she held her head up high and walked forward with a posture of confidence, knowing she could not afford the luxury of being seen as timid or weak. She prayed silently to the Gods, thanking them and pleading for their guidance in the coming weeks, months, and years.

Bersant stood watching the ceremony next to King Agron, who was dressed in an astonishing array of gold and silver. In full sun he might have blinded a man, but the evening light made him glow like embers of a fire. Teuta was presented with a diamond necklace placed on a large red pillow—a symbol of her new stature as Queen of Illyria. Agron stood hand on his sword, crown on his head, and a smile that stretched across the Kingdom.

As Taulant and Teuta approached, Agron removed his sword and knelt before them. Presenting the sword to Taulant, he asked him to swear to protect Illyria and his daughter until the end of his days.

The ceremony was filled with grand words, countless fanfares, and elaborate rituals, each having a purpose or a meaning that was mostly lost on Teuta. After more than an hour and a half, they all led to the final promise.

King Agron and Queen Teuta faced each other and spoke. "It is with one mind and one heart that we humbly give our most sacred honor to all Illyrians, that we will love, cherish, and protect the Kingdom and our families until our last breath. This is our pledge, our BESA. Guided by our ancestors and by each and every tribe, we give our BESA freely and with full knowledge of the sacredness of our words."

Bersant turned to King Agron. "Do you give your Besa to Teuta?

"Po," he replied.

"Do you, Queen Teuta, give your Besa to Agron, King of Illyria?

"Po," she replied.

Bersant turned to the crowd, raising the sword of Agron high above his head. "Are you all witness to the Besa?"

"Po," the crowd roared, their voices echoing up and down the corridors of the castle as they shouted the Illyrian word for approval and confirmation.

"Let the Gods offer a merciful death if the Besa is broken." Bersant turned back to Agron and Teuta. "From this moment, you are Queen Teuta of Illyria, wife of King Agron. And you are King Agron, sworn husband of Queen Teuta. May your union be fruitful and your rule just. Let the wine flow and music play and fill this night with joy for all Illyria."

Bersant paused for the couple to consummate their union with a kiss. And the crowd once again filled the air with "Po, Po, Po!"

Agron beamed down at Teuta. "I love you, my Queen." She smiled. "I love you, my King."

The crowd converged on them with congratulations and bestowed them with gifts, each and every citizen taking their turn.

The music was joyous and dancing ensued.

"Shall we dance?" Agron bowed to Teuta.

"Yes, my King." She gave him her hand and they slowly began stepping with the music.

The wedding festivities lasted into the early hours of the morning, and the bells rang throughout the Kingdom, announcing that Illyria had a new Queen.

AFTER AN ETERNITY, AGRON and Teuta found themselves alone, away from the crowds and from the festivities. Agron looked down at the woman lying in his arms, and once again his breath was taken away. "I want you in my arms forever." They kissed and made passionate love on the rich silk sheets and opulent bed of their marriage chamber.

"Don't ever abandon me," Teuta whispered in the King's ear as she kissed his eyes, nose, cheeks, hair....

ALMOST THREE WEEKS PASSED. Agron and Teuta had spent much of that time getting to know every inch of their bodies and the depth of their souls. After a day or two in bed, they would rise and take to the practice field, sparring with the same passion as their lovemaking, falling breathless and laughing to the ground after the vigorous exercise. They lived in their own world, spoke their own language, and no one dared disturb them. Dora and Norik performed their duties silently, usually when Agron and Teuta were fast asleep and dreaming. The early days of their marriage were a time of bliss, where the world seemed far away. Yet the world had gone on.

During those early weeks, Arion had succeeded in conquering the Dardan tribe but paid a high price for his success, losing more than five hundred soldiers during the first day. Macedonian forces were at their limit as dead bodies, swords, arrows, and blood littered the battlefield.

Arion summoned a messenger, handing him a letter accompanied by the command, "Ride as you have never ridden before, and give this message to King Agron." At once, the messenger mounted his horse and sped off.

Arion could have been proud of his military accomplishment, but he was concerned at the loss of so many men. They were King Agron's men, and he was responsible for them. He also knew he would have a difficult time fending off any enemy advances in such a weakened state. With the Macedonians stretched to the limit, he had no option but to seek the King's help.

NORIK KNOCKED ON THE King's Chamber door. It was late afternoon, yet he had heard not even a hint of stirring from the King and Queen. He knew his interruption would not be welcome, but he also knew that the message from Arion was of vital importance.

"My Lord, he whispered through the door."

At first there was no reply, not a sound. He tried again. "I apologize, my King, but a messenger has brought a letter from Arion."

The room seemed to spring to life with a cacophony of sounds. Suddenly the door swung open, displaying the King standing tall but only half-dressed. Without a word, he extended his hand for the letter, which Norik handed him. The King read it and handed it back, then glanced to the bed where Queen Teuta was lounging, then turned back to Norik.

"Prepare my horse and alert my lieutenants." He shut the door as Norik acknowledged his orders with a "Yes, my Lord."

Queen Teuta looked concerned as the King began to dress. "What is it? Is it so important that you must leave our wedding bed?"

Agron leaned over and kissed her lips. "Do not worry, my Queen. I will be gone only a few days. Arion, my commander, is fighting a battle with the Etoil and Dardan tribes and needs my reinforcements. I am sorry I have to leave you."

Teuta suddenly flashed back to her dream about Agron, and a cold shiver rose up her spine. "Don't go."

"But I must. I am the King…. My army needs me, my kingdom needs me." He kissed her passionately, with all his might, and she returned his kiss as if the world were going to end.

Agron drew back to take in her full beauty. "Wait for me, my love."

"I will always wait for you." Teuta's eyes watered unexpectedly, for she had never felt such emotion before.

Agron reached up and touched her tears. "I go with you in my heart, your scent on my mind, your touch always on my cheek, and your tears on my fingertips. Wait for me." Then he turned and left the chambers.

Teuta moved to the window to watch him mount his horse and ride away, her jaw set and her demeanor resolute. She would not let false dreams or superstition bend her thoughts. Still, she needed reassurance and went searching for Norik.

She found him as Norik was returning from the stables. He was surprised to see her.

"Is there something wrong, my Queen?"

"Norik, tell me, how many guards ride with the King?"

"Forty, my Lady." He saw her concern and was quick to try to dispel any unwarranted fears. "My Queen, he will be safe. He has seen more than one hundred wars and knows his way around a battle. He will return in a few days. Is there something I can do for you to take your mind off of his departure?"

"Yes," Teuta replied, taking Norik up on his offer. "I need lots of arrows, a place to practice, and to see my father."

Taulant was summoned to the archery practice field where Teuta was dressed in her hunting clothes furiously loosing arrows at the targets.

"Daughter, is now the right time to practice your skills? Shouldn't you be settling into your chambers and organizing your court?"

Teuta stopped just long enough to reply, "My chambers are empty, my King has gone off to fight a war, and I am left here with handmaidens and housework." She loosed another arrow that struck the center of the 10-inch-thick target with such force that it penetrated straight through.

"The King must do what his station requires. He must lead, just as you must do what you are required to and be a comfort to him when he returns."

"What if he does not return?"

Taulant shook his head as Teuta gathered her arrows for another round. "Don't be foolish, child."

He followed her. "You must learn the noble ways with the same fervor you learned to be a soldier. It is what is demanded of you now."

"I have had a dream, Father. A powerful and disturbing dream. It came to me the day after I met Agron. It was a dream of Agron fighting and being taken by angels. I shiver at the memory of it."

"The King fights many wars. Dying on the battlefield would be an honor for him, but that does not mean the current battlefield is the one in your dreams. What your dream envisions could take place many years from now."

"I would rather my love die in my arms than on the cold ground. Your words do little to comfort me." Once again, she shot arrows at the targets.

KING AGRON AND HIS men approached the battlefield. Arion and Demetrius rode to greet them.

"Welcome, my King. Your arrival will lift spirits and urge our forces forward." Arion pointed to the Illyrian soldiers scattered across a low field.

"What is the situation?" asked the King, even as he could already see flaws in the dispersing of his men. Yet, he patiently listened.

"I lost one hundred more men," Arion lamented. "The enemy fights like wild lions...."

The King raised his hand to stop Arion. "I want to hear your solution, not the problem. I can see that your men are too scattered, too spread out to make any significant advance."

"We are trying to hold ground, my King." Arion's horse pawed the ground restlessly.

"What we need to do is to surround them, not wallow in a damp field waiting for their advance. Gather the soldiers, have them flank the sides and send the archers down the middle."

Arion blinked and Demetrius was already halfway to the men.

As Demetrius's men drove forward, the enemy forces countered, pushing back the advancing Illyrians to the lowlands, where Agron and Arion's forces united to make a counter-attack, sending a storm of arrows that decimated the enemy forces. Motivated by their King's presence, the Illyrians fought even harder, sacrificing their hearts, their souls, and their bodies on the field of battle. After many hours of fierce fighting and at the cost of many of their soldiers, the Illyrians prevailed.

As the Illyrian army retreated, wounded enemy soldiers screamed for their kinsmen, who had long disappeared into the woods. Thousands lay dead and dying. The victorious King Agron never got used to the sight; it always unnerved him, and he always prayed to the Gods that every man be accepted into the heavenly realm upon death.

The soldiers hailed their King's leadership, and he declared a night of revelry while he rested for his return journey. Grateful that the battle was over, Agron yearned to head back to his Queen.

THE EVENING WAS UPON them when the King heard loud voices and scuffling of feet outside his tent. The guards were not in their places, which put him on alert. As the commotion neared, Agron retrieved his sword and prepared for battle. Suddenly, Arion burst through the tent flaps, hauling a boy behind him by his collar. The boy struggled but Arion held tight.

"I just want to pay tribute to the King, to hug him, and give him a present," whimpered the boy.

"What is all this?" Agron asked as the boy cowered in front of him.

"Just a hug. I am eager to know my King, to pay tribute."

The boy reminded Agron of his son. He was the same age and equal in height.

"Come closer, boy." But Arion held him back, even as he resisted, and the guards closed in, prepared for any deceit.

"Where did you find this boy?" the King asked.

"This lad eluded the outer guards and was passing the stables when I spotted him."

Agron leaned toward the boy, who turned his face to the ground, finally settling down, stopping resistance to his capture.

"Where are you from?"

"North."

"North? Just North? And what has brought you here this evening?"

"I heard there was to be a great battle, and I wanted to witness it for myself. I intend to be a soldier when I am old enough."

Arion loosened his grip on the boy but still held his shirt. "He says you are his hero, after seeing how you won the battle today, and he wanted to hug the great King of Illyria."

"Battles are not to be praised, or witnessed," the King chastised. "They are horrid sights and better avoided if possible. A King should be praised for keeping peace, not for waging war."

The boy looked up at the King, his eyes tearing and the corners of his mouth quivering.

The King gave him a sympathetic glance. "What is your name? How old are you?"

"Tristan, my King. I am 14 years old."

Agron motioned for the boy to come nearer. Simultaneously, the guards moved closer as well, but the King waved them off.

"Tristan, I hope you grow up in a time of peace and prosperity. Would you like something to eat? You must be hungry after your journey from the North."

The boy retreated a few steps as Agron held out a piece of meat. "Here, I am not feeling hungry. Take mine."

The boy's eyes grew big, and Agron could tell he hadn't eaten in days. Still, the boy hesitated and looked around the room filled with men covered in the gore of battle.

Agron saw the fear in the boy's eyes and opened his arms, inviting Tristan to receive the hug he so desired. The boy kept his eyes to the ground as he embraced the King. It felt good to be enfolded in the arms of a soldier, a feeling he had never encountered before now. It was a feeling that almost made him forget his purpose.

But then he straightened and drew a dagger from his sleeve. "This is for my father, whom you murdered last night." With eyes wide in anger, he plunged the knife into Agron's back. Agron jerked backward, screaming in pain, and flung Tristan from him. The boy scrambled to escape, but the guards were on him in an instant. They held him to the ground as he struggled. One of the guards raised the boy's head up, then slit his throat. It was over in a moment, and the cry went out across the encampment. "The King has been attacked!"

Arion rushed to Agron's side. He tried to stop the bleeding with his hands, but the knife had gone deep and punctured a lung. Agron was awake but had trouble speaking. He grabbed at Arion's cloak and gurgled, "Home, take me home."

"We must not move you, my Lord, until we stop the bleeding." Arion motioned to a physician, who had just arrived, to take over applying pressure on the wound.

A half hour passed, and the pile of blood-soaked rags grew. The physician finally arose and walked over to Arion who was pacing nearby. "My Lord," he began, wiping blood from his hands.

"Speak to me."

"He is dire, the knife went deep, and we cannot stop the bleeding. I have sent for some witch hazel and turmeric. He is weak and must not be moved."

Helplessly defiant, Arion protested, "I have the King's orders. We will be moving him in the morning. You have to stop the bleeding." He did not wait for a response, leaving the doctor to attend to the preparations of transporting the King.

IT WAS EIGHT O'CLOCK in the morning when Teuta bolted upright in her bed, screaming. Her hair was matted with sweat and her body shook. Dora came flying into her chamber, and Norik arrived a few moments later. Teuta was breathing heavily, eyes wide with fear.

Dora stopped abruptly. "What is it, my Queen?"

Teuta grabbed Dora's sleeve. "The King," she moaned, as Dora tried to comfort her.

"What about the King, my Lady?"

Norik brought over a flask of water.

"Something has happened. I feel it, I know it."

Norik urged her to drink. "It was just a dream, my Queen."

"He was calling to me; he needs my help," Teuta insisted, rising from her bed and beginning to dress. Norik and Dora watched helplessly as she slipped on her shoes and picked up her bow.

"There has been no such news, my Queen," Norik cautioned. "It is foolish to go riding off when you don't even know where you should be going."

"The Gods will guide me." And she ran the door toward the stable.

TEUTA RODE HARD THROUGH the day's gloom, which hung like a shroud over the landscape. Her black hair streamed wild behind her. More than an hour passed before she came upon Agron's guards riding just as hard toward Epidamnus. When they saw Teuta, they stopped and informed her that the King wasn't far behind—that they were clearing the way so they could get to the Castle as soon as possible.

Teuta saw the gravity of the situation on the faces of the men as she approached Agron's litter. Arion and Demetrius flanked the King on either side, clearly startled by the new Queen's presence.

Dismounting from her horse, Teuta ran to her King. "My darling, my love, what has happened?"

Agron was in a delirium. His face was sickly pale and his hands cold as she clutched them.

"My husband, let me tend to you." She peered at the wound and quickly realized the gravity of the situation.

Agron turned his head in recognition of Teuta's voice. "My Queen, I wanted to see your face one more time."

"Hush, my love."

"I am sorry…. I am sorry. Thank you for your love…. It has changed my life and given me hope for the future of our land. Be kind to Rron… he is too young…. You will be the Queen of Illyria…. My Queen…. I Love You…." Agron's words became more and more faint, his body growing weaker by the second. Yet he somehow gathered his strength and composure to utter his last wishes to his betrothed: "You will rule with the same heart that has bonded with mine…. I need your Besa one more time."

"Shhh, my King. You must save your breath. I am not ready for you to go. You will not go." Tears welled up in her eyes.

"The Gods have already given me a taste of paradise. I must go with them. I am thankful they led me to you…. Remember me…." His words were now mere whispers. "Give me your Besa so I can go."

Teuta sobbed as she said the words. "I give you my Besa, again and again and again. Besa Po, my love, my King."

The King smiled, touched her face, and closed his eyes to enter the endless dream.

CHAPTER THREE

QUEEN TEUTA: BORN TO LEAD

T HE SUN CROSSED THE afternoon sky, and Teuta was still in bed with the curtains closed, shimmering shards of light darting through. Three days had passed since the burial of her beloved King. She did not understand how the Gods could be so cruel as to put her in the arms of her love and then rip him away so quickly.

With barely time to mourn, she was immediately beset by the issues of the Realm—most urgently, who was to rule in succession. She had told the court the King's wishes, what he had said to her that night, but there were those who challenged her, including Apollonia and Arion. The court called on Scerdilaidas to apply since he was Agron's brother, but he had little interest in the idea of ruling. At the same time, he was vocal about who should not rule. He had long seen the influence that Arion had on his brother and the power he had been granted. He did not trust Arion's Besa, and the fact that

Arion had been close to Apollonia for many years before she married Agron stuck in Scerdilaidas' throat when he thought of it. Arion had had good counsel with Teuta, and it seemed she trusted him.

Scerdilaidas spoke with Teuta into the night and revealed much to her that she did not know about the Kingdom and its leaders. Some of the information surprised her and some did not. The conversation left her head swimming, thoughts bouncing hither and yon, and it took her a long time to fall asleep.

"I t's late, my queen. May I open the curtains?"

Teuta waved at Dora to go away.

"Would you like something to eat?" Dora continued.

"Leave me alone."

"Your father is here and wants to talk with you. Apollonia has been by, but I sent her away."

"I have a terrible headache. Can't you just let me be?"

At that moment, her father stepped through the door; he had not waited for permission to enter his daughter's chambers. Horrified by Teuta's appearance, he took a step backward.

"You look terrible," he bellowed.

"I know, Father. I simply want to be gone from this life; all the joy I felt, the happiness I experienced has been ripped away. All that is left is my promise, my Besa, but how am I supposed to fulfill it? To be Queen of Illyria?" She tried to retreat to a dark corner of the room.

"My heart is breaking…. For you to become both a Queen and a widow in less than a month…. I understand how hard it is for you." He went to comfort his daughter, and she did not refuse. They embraced for a long moment.

Taulant's tenderness filled the room. "I know it is hard, but you must be strong for all of Illyria. Everyone will be looking to see what you will do. Surprise them. If they expect you to wear black, choose another color. Mourn your beloved husband by making what he has built even better. Ready yourself to conquer all the tribes, to stand up to the Roman Empire. The King's spirit will be with you, always."

Teuta resisted his words, but in the end, she nodded in assent. "I love you, Father; would you tell Dora that I need to see her when you leave?"

"Certainly. You will be a great leader, my daughter. Songs will be written and stories will be told about you. Your name will live for eternity." And then he left.

Teuta stared into the mirror endlessly, as if trying to convince herself to believe her father's words.

ARION WAS CONSTANTLY AT Rron's side, urging him to be involved in the art of war. Inviting him to join his men, to travel throughout the Kingdom and see for himself that everything was in order, even make changes if he felt like it.

But Rron would have none of it. "The Kingdom and I are still mourning. My heart is bleeding because I never had a chance to say goodbye to my father. Now I am supposed to help the Kingdom? I can barely help myself or take care of my mother. I must stay close to her now that Queen Teuta is my official guardian. Who else will take care of her?"

"I understand that you are mourning, Rron, but you must be stronger now. You must see the world. As for your mother, I will look after her, as I always have. She will never be alone." The set of Arion's jaw relayed his resoluteness.

"Why can't my uncle Scerdilaidas be the one to handle official duties? Besides, the Queen doesn't like me." Rron sulked in his chair.

"I don't think your assessment of the Queen's feelings about you is accurate, and Scerdilaidas has no interest in becoming King. Since Teuta is Queen, she is rightfully the one to rule while you still maintain your status as heir until you become of age and undertake the Kingship. Now is when you must prepare for the day when you become King of Illyria." Rron reluctantly took the short sword Arion handed him just as Apollonia entered the room.

She glared at Arion. "What is going on here?"

"The boy needs to be trained."

"Not today he doesn't." She took Rron by the hand and started dragging him out of the room, forcing him to drop the sword.

"This is not good for the Kingdom nor your son, my Lady." She did not answer as she hauled Rron off.

THE ENEMIES OF ILLYRIA were celebrating. With Rron, who was only a boy, and Teuta, an unexperienced young woman, many believed the Kingdom was especially vulnerable, and they were eager to take advantage of the situation. Bersant came to visit the Queen, wanting to be on record as the one to inform her of the threat.

"They will slowly get to your Generals, then Arion and Demetrius, and the Kingdom will fall apart," he warned, seeming to take pleasure in his prediction.

Teuta scowled at him. "Let them come. They have no idea who I am and what I am capable of."

Bersant smiled. "I can feel your anger. You have spirit, I will give you that. But it will take more than spirit to keep our enemies at bay. King Agron knew when to be diplomatic and when to wage war. It was something bred in him. You...."

"I am the daughter of a warrior, a General who taught me well, but you knew that. Both of you served the same master, and now you come here trying to gain power by giving advice that is neither needed nor wanted. When my enemies gather against me, will you then give me counsel, or will you join them to be rid of me?"

"My Queen, I am a servant of Illyria. I do not seek personal gain or power; my time for both has passed, and I implore you to consider what I have said. Even the strongest of rulers need sage advice. I apologize if I seem too forward in my remarks. I only wish to be of service." He bowed deeply, but Teuta was still wary of his motives.

"I accept your apology, and I will heed what you say, but do not mistake my lack of practical experience for naiveté. I want a full accounting of the Kingdom's wealth in gold, weapon stores, and maps of the Kingdom and surrounding areas. Oh, and set up a meeting with my generals for this afternoon." Bersant nodded, bowed again, and left without another word.

Dora stood waiting by the door, bowing to Bersant as he left, then turning to Teuta. "The tailors have arrived and are ready for you."

Seething at the Queen's reprimand and her assignment of a task that was far beneath him, Bersant stormed down the hallway. *I am not your lackey to be calling meetings*, he fumed. He needed to do as she ordered for now but in a way so as not to lose face with his peers. *Ah*, he realized, *giving the information about the meeting to Arion would be just as good as telling everyone himself.* He smiled.

T HE CASTLE, STILL IN mourning, was quiet. Fountains echoed through the noiseless halls, soft sobs of women could be heard behind closed doors, and the kitchen staff prepared meals in silence. Rron lay curled in his bed, eyes wet from crying. Arion entered his room and sat on the bed, looking down on him.

"You must get up; the Queen has summoned you. You have to act like royalty, not a sniveling servant." Disturbed by Arion's tone, Rron sat up. Arion had never talked to him that way before.

"Norik is waiting for you, dry your eyes and straighten your clothes." Rron rose from the bed, wiping his eyes with his sleeve.

"I have the right to mourn. Why are you speaking this way to me?"

Arion tossed him his cloak. "A King knows what is expected of him and does not wallow in self-pity. You must grow up now and fast."

Without a further word, Norik led Rron and Arion to Queen Teuta's quarters. The Queen, dressed in a white gown with bunted sleeves, was practicing with King Agron's sword, lunging and parrying at an invisible foe. She paused to welcome them.

"Thank you for coming. It is time we got to know each other better. And the best way to do that is to train together."

"My Lady?" Arion was unclear what she meant.

"As of tomorrow, we shall call upon the best swordsmen, we shall summon the finest archers of the Kingdom, and we shall begin training, here in the gardens if need be. We will practice every day. There is no time to waste. Our Kingdom depends on us being strong. Body and mind. Rron, you will be schooled by our best scholars until your knowledge becomes unparalleled." Rron looked at her, overwhelmed.

"Oh, and Norik, I would like to have breakfast with Queen Apollonia tomorrow as well." She turned back to Arion and Rron with a smile. "I look forward to our training."

"My Queen." Arion sensed his influence in the court was in jeopardy, and he wanted to gain some ground.

"I have been training Rron, and as I happen to be the best swordsman in the Castle, I would like to continue his training. There may be some things I can show Your Excellency as well."

Teuta looked at Arion for a moment. "We need to be trained by the best swordsman in the Kingdom, not in the Castle," she stated. "I have summoned such a person, and I am sure there are some things you can learn from him as well." Arion bristled but kept his mouth shut.

"Arion, I am not here to make a personal affront against you. You are a valued member of my court, but I have to think of what is best for the Kingdom, not worry about any individual's conceits."

"Understood, my Queen. I apologize if I seemed defensive. I have known Rron since birth and feel a kinship with him."

Teuta nodded and turned to Norik. "I will give you a handsome reward for expediting my requests." Norik bowed and left. Arion and Rron followed.

As they walked the Castle halls back to their chambers, Arion confided in Rron that he was at once impressed and fearful of what Queen Teuta would do in the coming days. It was clear she could not be easily manipulated nor intimidated. Yet he felt that his duty to Rron and Apollonia must not be undermined or threatened even by the Queen. His place in the ruling hierarchy may have been diminished, but he still had loyal followers and knew that he must come up with a strategy.

QUEEN APOLLONIA HAD OUTDONE herself, dressing in her best attire, her hair coiffed as if she were going to a wedding, such as the one she had deliberately missed—that of Teuta and Agron. She wore her most prized jewelry, the necklace Agron had given her on her wedding day. And bracelets bounced up the length of her wrists, making her skin barely visible.

Entering his mother's quarters, Rron was surprised to see her so elegantly dressed. "You look so beautiful, Mother. Is all this for Teuta?"

"I want to show her what a Queen looks like," replied his mother with a flourish of her arm and her most regal pose. She stood that way a moment for emphasis, then collapsed into a chair. "What does she want from me? I am nervous. Me!! Nervous! I pity her in a way. I don't think she has any idea what she is getting into. This den of cutthroats, this Kingdom of strife."

Rron tried to be subtle. "She wanders the Castle alone and does not heed her bodyguards' advice."

"She will learn or be devoured." Apollonia rose and strode to the mirror. She was adjusting her hair when Norik announced Teuta's arrival. Apollonia hurried to her seat and struck her pose.

"Enter," she exclaimed a little too quickly.

Rron stood behind her and fiddled with his jacket hem. He watched as Teuta crossed the threshold, dressed in the simple white dress that immediately either made Apollonia appear overdressed or Teuta underdressed for the occasion.

"I am honored that you have taken the time to see me in my quarters. I know how busy you must be." Apollonia's nervousness fueled her words.

Teuta walked over to embrace Apollonia. "You are so beautiful."

The new Queen seemed to be going out of her way to be pleasant to Apollonia. It threw the former Queen off guard.

"Thank you, Queen Teuta. You are very beautiful as well, as beautiful as an angel, Agron's father used to say."

"I am here simply to meet you, to relieve any tension or misinformation. I came into your life as an intruder. Now I would like to ask for your friendship. Especially in the present circumstances, it would be better if we worked together, helped each other protect the homeland that we both love, our Kingdom of Illyria."

Apollonia suddenly felt overdressed and attempted to subtly remove some of the garnishments in her hair. "Thank you, I have felt alone and melancholic after the death of King Agron. I worry for my son and who will take the firm reins that Agron held."

"I will rule in Rron's stead until he is old and wise enough to assume his father's place. We have to be strong; we cannot show fear to our enemies or any sign of weakness. I will fight with all my strength to keep the Kingdom safe and even stronger. I will fight with the strength of King Agron, for it is his spirit and the Gods that guide me. I gave my Besa for that."

Apollonia was seeing what Agron liked about this new Queen. She was certainly no fading flower and seemed to have the strength needed to succeed. It would be a fatal mistake to underestimate her. She decided in that moment to give the new Queen her support. Apollonia lifted a glass of wine that had been set before them at the beginning of their meeting and raised it to Teuta. "You can count on me."

Rron looked confused until his mother reached to embrace him. "It is my son who is the important one; I am merely a servant of his future and believe that you have his best interests at heart. For that, I thank you."

Queen Teuta left the room after another hour or so of talk, laughter, wine, and tears. She was relieved that she would not have to fight a battle with Apollonia within the Castle while fighting enemies without. That night she slept soundly for the first time since Agron's death.

ROME WATCHED WITH INTEREST as reports from Illyria came in. Leaders set a consul meeting to discuss plans in light of Agron's death. Attendees included Marcus Aemilius, a man of few words and profound appearance in his sixtieth year, with a silence full of schemes; Junius Pera, a tall, big-boned man and known womanizer who was said to keep more than twenty young girls as servants, changing them every six months. Still, his wisdom was admired among the Roman elite. These two men were joined by censors Valerius Flaccus, a short, rotund man with long hair, considered a puppet of Marcus, and Quintus Fabius Maximus, a handsome young man with short black hair and large hazel eyes. He was highly accomplished at a young age, and all the girls imagined him as their husband.

The consult attendees reclined on their large satin pillows, eating grapes and drinking wine out of silver cups, surrounded by beautiful women dancing to the lively music played by skilled musicians. They were celebrating.

Marcus raised his cup. "To King Agron and his timely demise."

"Cheers," everyone chimed in.

"Such a sad story, the fierce King dying from the blade of a child. You see, even the greatest of men can be done in by the passion of youth," Junius noted as he fondled and kissed one of the women in attendance.

"Yes, and within a week we can conquer Illyria if we send ten thousand soldiers and one hundred ships, attacking at their weakest moment." A chorus of cheers greeted Fabius's suggestion.

"The Kingdom with a child heir and a woman leading the battle. It will be the easiest war ever," Junius laughed as everyone joined in the mirth. "Oh, and I want Queen Teuta for myself. I hear she is very beautiful. I want her to wash me, to serve me with her body and lips." He cackled drunkenly.

"You have claimed her," Fabius proclaimed, raising his glass to seal the bargain.

The Illyrian Kingdom had long been a thorn in the side of the Roman Empire. Initially, Rome had thought Illyria was simply a nuisance, raiding their ships and stealing Roman goods, but as King Agron rose to power and conquered tribal territory increasingly close to the Roman Empire, Rome had started taking notice.

The Romans had yet to cross the Adriatic in a direct confrontation, but King Agron's death and the Kingdom's suspected weakness was emboldening them.

RETURNING TO EPIDAMNUS FROM Pharos with urgent news, Demetrius confided in Arion before approaching the Queen, still uncertain of her abilities even though they were cousins. They both decided to meet with Queen Teuta.

Teuta was standing on the balcony looking out over the city when the two arrived. She turned to them as they approached. Expecting only Arion to attend the meeting, she was surprised by Demetrius's presence but graciously greeted both of them. "It is good to see you, cousin…and General Arion." Both men bowed.

"You have news; otherwise why would two of my ranking officers come to see me as one?"

"Yes, my Queen," Arion answered.

Demetrius did not hesitate. "One of my informants has relayed a message that the Romans are sending a fleet of one hundred ships to invade Illyria. They are seizing on the death of Agron as an opportunity to strike."

"And so it begins…." She turned back to viewing the expanse of the city. "They believe us to be weak; they think that because a woman rules they can come to our shores at their pleasure." Anger tinged her voice as she turned back to the men. "Assemble the generals, one hour. We will see who is weak." Teuta brushed past the men without another word. The meeting was over.

IN HER CHAMBERS, TEUTA sat on the large bed while Dora laid out her battle clothes. She closed her eyes, trying to see Agron's face, to feel his arms, to summon his strength. She whispered, "Give me strength, my King." A warm breeze blew in the window, surrounding her, hugging her. It seemed to be saying, "My Queen, my Queen," and she knew that Agron was near. "I love you, my King. Give me courage and strength. Don't leave me."

"My Queen?" Dora said softly, trying not to break the spell that Teuta seemed to be under. "Everything is here." She pointed to the battle wear.

"These," Teuta selected, pointing to black leather leggings, an outer jacket with small pockets for knives on her shoulders, and short boots. *Finally, once again, she would be dressed in comfortable clothes.*

Generals from all reaches of the Kingdom along with the most esteemed advisors gathered in the great hall. Bersant was among them but kept his distance. Demetrius and Arion were in the front of the group still greeting latecomers when Teuta entered.

She waved a hand. "Good morning, all."

"Good morning," bellowed the crowd before becoming silent.

"It seems that the Roman Empire thinks we are weak. What do we say to that?" The generals roared and stamped their response, "No, No, No."

"They are sending a fleet of one hundred ships to our borders by way of Pharos and other islands. They will need two days to cross the Adriatic. I need a fleet of two hundred ships to defeat them. I will also need fifty ships with five hundred soldiers dressed as pirates to spread out along our waterways. The soldiers shall forego uniforms and instead don dark clothes and hide their faces. They shall attack the supply ships and steal their food, swords, arrows. I will command the Pirates, Arion the southern fleet, and Demetrius will head north to protect Pharos." The room filled with voices as each leader conferred on strategy and plans.

Designed by Teuta, a new banner was introduced to represent Illyria. It sported a red background with a black, two-headed eagle at the center.

Teuta explained, "This is our flag: red for the blood of Agron, the Eagle for our fierceness, and two heads with one body—I and my beloved King. We Illyrians are forces of the sea and coast, from east to west." She placed her hand over her heart and bowed her head. Everyone else followed suit.

"We will meet again after we defeat the Romans. BESA PO," Teuta called out triumphantly. "BESA PO," echoed the group as they filed out of the hall.

BESA PO

D EMETRIUS RODE ALONGSIDE QUEEN Teuta, leading
her five hundred guards and soldiers. They were headed toward
Pharos for the first time since she had met Agron and her life was
forever changed.

"Cousin," Demetrius began. "I fear for you in the pirate
ships. A Queen should be safe on her throne and not in the heart of
danger." He seemed genuinely concerned, although it was not lost
on Teuta that he had been consolidating his power in Pharos and the
surrounding islands.

"I will be fine. I have five hundred men to look after me," she
smiled. "The Consuls of Rome do not fear me yet, but they will. They
will know the strength of my love for Illyria and King Agron." She
winked at Demetrius, then rode back to be with her troops.

Their arrival in Pharos sparked much excitement and chaos
as the citizens tended to their needs and the needs of the Illyrian army. Most were glad to be of service, though a few grumbled
and complained.

By nightfall, the ships were ready, and all crew and soldiers
wore black outfits, successfully camouflaging themselves against the
night sky, making it difficult for them to even see each other when
the moon was hidden.

About a mile or two out, just off the coast, lay the Roman ships
resting before the morning attack. Voices from the enemy ships could
be heard as the Illyrians slowly approached. They used hand signals
to communicate while preparing their swords and arrows. As Teuta
gave General Gentius the order to attack, a hulking, muscled brute
of a man stood close to protect her, but she did not need protecting.

Some Roman guards had gotten wind of the attack, but it was too late; their cries were muffled, then silenced by the onslaught. Without hesitation, Teuta jumped into the battle, her sword cutting flesh and bone. Men approached her thinking she was just another soldier, until they were close enough to see her face. Then they would stop as if caught in a trance, making them easy targets to cut down as their surprise quickly turned to fear.

The battle lasted for many hours. The screams of Roman soldiers could be heard throughout the night as ships burned. Teuta claimed many Roman lives that night while her own pirates suffered few casualties. Her skills with the sword were far above those of most men and by the time the fight was over she had demonstrated her fierceness to the enemy and her own men.

The following morning Queen Teuta and her fleet returned to Pharos to rest and celebrate. Her ships were laden with much food, weapons, and valuables taken from the Romans. Teuta instructed General Gentius to distribute the food to the poor and store the weapons for further use.

The next morning, Demetrius and his army waited for the Roman invasion, but no ships appeared.

Prepared for battle, Demetrius was disappointed that he had been sent so far from the conflict; he wondered if his cousin had done so on purpose. Discovering that Teuta and her band of pirates had defeated the Roman fleet and claimed the glory did not sit well with him. Even more so when news of Queen Teuta's victory traveled throughout Illyria, securing her place as the rightful leader. Demetrius felt betrayed and angry.

Teuta knew that her victory would cause bad feelings, so she intentionally avoided claiming the victory as hers alone. Instead, she praised all the generals and soldiers who took part in the battle. She felt there was no sense in making too much from one fateful encounter with the enemy still gathered across the sea.

CONSUL JUNIUS RAGED AS he gathered all the Roman Generals. "You were defeated by a woman!!" He slammed his fist into the arm of his chair, and his face turned crimson. "A woman! How can this be?"

General Claudius Marcellus stepped forward. He had been decorated more than once for his victories, so Junius allowed him to speak.

"We underestimated Queen Teuta as a leader and deadly fighter. I saw firsthand how she slayed numerous Roman soldiers. She is as skilled as she is beautiful."

Junius interjected. "There is no excuse for being battered by any foe. We are Romans. We will bide our time, but be assured we will conquer the Illyrians." All the generals bowed their heads in agreement.

QUEEN TEUTA SPENT A few days at her father's house on Pharos to rest after the battle, then headed to Rhizon where Rron was staying with his uncle Prince Darsej and his aunt Doruntina.

While Teuta was eager to meet her new family, she was also interested in the possibility of establishing a castle on Pharos, a place that did not hold the bittersweet memories of King Agron and her awkward beginning as Queen.

Upon arrival, she was met by Scerdilaidas, Rron, and Prince Darsej, who was much younger then she had imagined. He had narrow eyes, brown hair and beard, and seemed amiable and without pretense. All three greeted her warmly, and Rron eagerly beckoned her to come see his new sword-fighting skills. Demetrius, Gentius, and other guards joined them for a celebration feast where both wild and true stories were told and laughter shared.

The next morning, Teuta arose early, forcing her still hungover and groggy attendants and guards to rise with her. She wanted to take a look around, to see the lay of the land and the feasibility of establishing a castle there.

CHAPTER FOUR

FORT AGRON

ARION, WHO HAD WAITED in the south for an attack that never came, finally returned to Epidamnus. Not seeing action and not being able to prove himself in battle frustrated him. He was also tired from his journey. Norik greeted him and asked if he wanted to see Queen Apollonia, who was anxious for news. Arion declined the invitation, deciding to wait until morning after a good night's sleep, when perhaps he would be less out of sorts. He knew that an encounter with the Queen would not go well at the moment.

Dressed in a lavish purple gown with lacy sleeves, Apollonia brushed her long red hair in the morning sunshine. The day was beautiful and she was happy, having received word that Arion had returned, though she wished he had come to her immediately upon his arrival. She was sure that today they would see each other once again. Her feelings for him had only grown stronger in his absence.

When Norik stopped by her chambers to tell her about Rron and his meeting with Queen Teuta, she inquired about Arion.

"He returned last night, exhausted," Norik informed her. "He went right to his quarters to rest. He asked about you and mentioned he would visit you this morning."

Anticipating Arion's visit, Apollonia strolled through the garden and down to the beach. While meandering, she remembered when she and Arion were young and collected flat stones for skipping over the tranquil water of the Castle pond. She knew that Arion would look for her there, since it had been a favorite place of theirs since childhood.

Soon she spotted Arion approaching from far down the beach, a figure in shining battle dress becoming more and more distinct. She let him draw near without acknowledgement until he was close, her heart beating louder by the second and her face flushing.

"Good morning, Queen Apollonia. I searched all over the Castle for you. Then I remembered our walks on the beach."

"Good morning, Arion. I have been worried for you and for this war. My eyes have scarcely dried from crying."

"My only concern these past days was being able to return to you, my Queen." Arion took Apollonia's hands in his. She shivered and brought her gaze to his. "I have hoped beyond hope," Arion continued, "that through these years you have found the love for me that I have for you. I have always loved you. The day you wedded Agron was the saddest day of my existence. Life is too short to take for granted what I feel for you."

Apollonia's knees were weak and her lips quivering. "I came here today to remind myself of the joyous days we spent together, when I first knew I loved you and always would." Arion could not believe his ears.

"Why hide your feelings all these years? Even after Agron's death?"

"When I was married to Agron, I could not break my Besa, and after his death it was too soon. But now, now we can finally be together."

They embraced and kissed passionately, freeing an imprisoned love. The night heard their ecstasy and left them helpless in each other's arms.

O N THE WAY BACK to Epidamnus, Queen Teuta returned to Pharos and her father's house. Her meeting with Rron and Prince Darsej had gone well, and she was eager to tell the only surviving member of her own family about it. They met in the dining hall of the old farmhouse that was strewn with the memories of her past.

Teuta opened the conversation, "Father, I understand now the sacrifice you made to raise me by yourself. You could have married after my mother's death, made your life easier, and had companionship in your older years. Why did you go through everything alone?"

Taulant glanced at her. He was preparing one of her favorite dishes. "The minute you were born and I saw your face while your mother was dying, I promised her and myself to take care of you until my last breath. I knew that you were special. Parents feel that sort of thing. I knew the Gods had brought you to this earth with a mission. I just didn't know what kind of a mission. Now I see. You came to save our Kingdom. I am sorry that it is such a hard mission. The hardest that the Gods can give. But it is one of the biggest honors, and I am more than a proud father. Still, I want you to consider getting married again. I want you to feel the divine feeling of a parent for a child."

Teuta reflected on her father's wishes for her. "My destiny is what the Gods have made it. You remain my one and only true family, and I love you beyond love. I am grateful for your sacrifices, yet King Agron was my other half; he was and will always be with me, in me, around me.... No other man's hand will be allowed to touch me. I know that I must make this sacrifice. Still, I have many children. They are all mine in a way. All the children of the Kingdom of Illyria. The Illyrians that I fight for, for their land, for their future, for their history. I am sorry to disappoint you, Father. Our paths are set, and neither of us can change that." Teuta held his hands and kissed them many times.

"I respect your mission, my child, and the Gods' immortal plan." Taulant handed Teuta her plate, and as they had for many years, they sat down together, alone in the house of Teuta's birth.

After a couple of days rest, Teuta was ready to return to Epidamnus, if just to confer with her consorts and advisors about her plans. It seemed, however, that her meeting on the Rhizon had stirred up some concerns. Both Prince Darsej and Bersant rode up to the farm as her guards were preparing her horse.

"Good day, my Queen," Bersant cooed. "We thought it prudent to meet with you before your return to the Castle."

"My dear Prince, and Master Bersant. I am surprised to see you both here together, given that you've obviously traveled from separate directions."

Bersant made an effort to keep the story casual. "Actually, I found the castle quite boring after you left, so I assembled some guards and traveled to Rhizon. I must have just missed you. When I told Prince Darsej I was looking to meet up with you, he decided to come along."

But Teuta sensed another motive. Clearly, Prince Darsej had no other motive than to be helpful, but Bersant was quick to take advantage of this to further his own ends.

"What is it that you wanted to talk about so urgently that it couldn't wait until my return to Epidamnus?" Teuta asked as politely as she could muster.

"I have it on authority that you might not return to the Castle, that you seek to establish a new Capital. I am curious about the veracity of the information and, if it is true, what assistance I may be in accomplishing your endeavor." Bersant had carefully chosen his words, but their real meaning was transparent: *It goes against every fiber of your being to be out of touch with the inner workings of the Realm, and being so isolated in castle Epidamnus made you nervous. Just admit your addiction to power and influence. I would judge you less harshly if you were truthful rather than making half-handed attempts at assistance you have no power to grant.*

Teuta saw Prince Darsej putting up his hands, recusing himself of the conversation. She smiled. "Yes, I have a plan. Had you been patient, I would have consulted with you in due time."

Bersant pursed his lips but dared not speak again. "Since the Romans have chosen to enter our borders here, near the Rhizon, I thought it wise to build a new Castle to prepare for the Roman Galleys approaching. Near Pharos there is a place called Sucuraj. It is there that I intend to erect my new Capital. Sucuraj has a deep bay and is surrounded by hills. We can place warships in such a way as to be almost invisible to the Romans and soldiers on top of the hills, to monitor traffic and attack swiftly if necessary. We will have the advantage and be able to subdue all Roman ships. It will be called Fort Agron."

Bersant was visibly upset; his plan was veering off course. Obviously, this Queen was not to be crossed. He weighed his options as Taulant's serving boy arrived with wine and sweets. Bersant drank deeply while Prince Darsej held his cup without taking a sip.

"I also want to order five large warships," she continued. "They shall be called 'The Liburnia' and will display my symbols showing our fierceness and power."

Teuta reached for a cup of wine and took a drink. As soon as she did, Prince Darsej finally lifted his cup to drink too. She noted his act of respect and toasted to him. "I will send my best craftsmen and laborers to help build the Castle. I can also offer you shipwrights if you so desire."

Prince Darsej returned the toast while Bersant asked for more wine.

"Of course, your help is welcome," Teuta inserted. "We will need all the help we can get to keep the Romans from taking our land," she added graciously.

THROUGHOUT THE SUMMER AND the fall, thousands of workers from across Illyria cut trees, hewed stones from the hills, and constructed Teuta's new Castle. Timbers from the hinterland forests joined forces to become warships, and by late autumn, the new ship Liburnia was near completion. Throughout the months, bands of Illyrian pirates set upon Roman ships and safely slipped back to the hidden port.

Queen Apollonia and Arion were pleased to manage Epidamnus and were not concerned that Rron spent most of his time with Teuta at the new Castle. As the days progressed, he grew stronger and fonder of the new Queen.

One day, Rron decided to pay Teuta a visit expressly to thank her for making a place for him in the new Castle; he entered her chambers as if they were his own.

"Rron!" Teuta exclaimed. "How are you doing?"

Rron was sincere in his gratitude. "I want to thank you for your generosity. I feel I am making a contribution to the Kingdom now."

"Don't be silly, my boy. I am your regent and you are the heir to the Kingdom. I serve your future and only your future. You have worked hard. It is a credit to you, your mother, and your father that you are growing up to be such a fine man."

Rron smiled shyly.

"When the Castle is finished," Teuta counseled him, "you should choose a beautiful girl and get married."

Rron blushed.

"I *was* in love," Rron mumbled, embarrassed and looking at the floor.

"Really? That is wonderful."

"Her name was Dorotea. My mother was against our being together because Dorotea was the daughter of a servant in the Castle.

Mother made them both leave. Ever since then, I have dreamed of her."

"Well, we must find her. You deserve to be happy. I will put the word out all over the Kingdom."

"You would do that?" Rron asked in amazement.

"Of course." Teuta called over a guard, whispered in his ear, and sent him away.

"Done. Life is too short to be without the one you love. You never know what tomorrow will bring." She smiled down on Rron.

"Thank you, Queen Teuta, but my mother is not going to be happy."

"Don't worry. I will talk to her. I am sure she will be moved by your love." She stroked his cheek and sent him away.

WINTER HAD SET IN and the rain poured down in Rome. Consul Fabius paced his chambers, furious, holding a message from his Illyrian spies.

He confronted Consul Postumius in the gallery. "That Illyrian witch and her pirates have attacked thirty of our ships. They have killed the soldiers and made off with food, wine, and gold. A trader found three warships stripped bare and abandoned on the sea. Something must be done. Each week, the Queen attacks more and more of our ships."

Postumius tried to calm Fabius and bring some perspective. "We are not at war; the sea is neutral. Yes, their attacks are reprehensible, but we must not overreact. Our empire is not threatened by a band of pirates. Perhaps we should send messengers to speak with her, negotiate an agreement to cease her raids on our property."

Fabius shook his head in disagreement, not convinced. "You have only to see her actions to know her intent. She thinks she can intimidate us. She is back at her Castle laughing...."

Postumius interrupted Fabius' rant. "If she does not listen to our terms and negotiate for peace, we will have to consider a war with Illyria, but not until diplomatic measures are taken. If the consul agrees, I will choose the messengers. We will have our answer one way or another."

BERSANT RETURNED TO EPIDAMNUS, simmering at the reception he had received from Teuta and his inability to curry favor with many of her consorts. He was not used to being ignored, so he decided to make himself as useful to Queen Apollonia and Arion as possible. In them, he immediately found a willing audience and the respect he was used to.

"It is an honor, Master Bersant, to have you with us again," Queen Apollonia said as Bersant entered her chambers.

"Thank you, my Queen. I come bearing news of your son, Rron, and Queen Teuta along with their best wishes and love."

"I am eager to hear all you have to tell." She invited him to sit beside her, ordered wine to be brought in, then eagerly listened.

Bersant began his report. "The Castle is being made of beautiful white stones with crafted wood interiors, including a large bedroom with thick, rose-colored curtains. A large space for meetings sits in the center where banquets can also be held. The artisans have created a large map of Illyria and the surrounding territories and have placed huge amphoras full of wine and water around the hall for the coming ceremonies."

"It sounds like Queen Teuta has good taste and intelligence to make a Castle so grand," Apollonia observed with a hint of envy, which Bersant noted for future reference. He decided to wait to tell her about Queen Teuta's search for Rron's Dorotea.

It is time, Bersant thought to himself, *that I look out for my own interests.* After serving Agron and his father for many years, they were both gone now, and with his station as advisor in jeopardy, playing his cards right could bring him the power and recognition he had long been denied.

"My Queen, I might have a way in which you can regain the power and prestige you once enjoyed."

Apollonia looked at Bersant with a flicker of interest. Although she was now an enthusiastic supporter of Teuta, Bersant saw an opportunity to change her position. He knew that the idea of regaining her status would give her pause, and he smiled.

T HE NEW CASTLE WAS complete and preparations were finally being made for Teuta to spend her first night in Fort Agron. The town was still under construction, but after months of working from Pharos, there was no time to waste in establishing her base of operations.

Taulant accompanied his daughter as they walked the Castle halls. "Are you happy?"

"I am as happy as I can be without the one I love by my side. I am happy being here with you." She took his hand and held it tight. He smiled.

"No stone or wood can replace the human heart." She hugged him.

As they headed back to the Grand Hall for the festivities, Demetrius approached. Teuta broke from her father's embrace and called out warmly to her cousin, "General…." She came up to him and walked by his side. "You bring news?" she asked.

"My Queen, I see you have placed your Castle and town in excellent strategic positions. You are wise." Demetrius bowed.

"Tell me, Demetrius, how many Roman ships have we conquered so far?'

"Fifty-eight ships, Your Majesty."

Teuta frowned. "That's not enough. We need to weaken the Empire even more. I want the borders of Illyria to reach Buzet and Pola, as close as we can get to the Roman Empire. I want them to see our strength and fear our armies, our navies."

Her determination was clear. Demetrius understood Teuta's desire to protect Illyria and knew she was capable of the task, yet he was of the opinion that to make Illyria stronger, it needed strong allies.

Teuta sensed his ambivalence. "I am grateful for your service, Cousin, and for bringing Agron to me. I hope I can count on your assistance in protecting Illyria and Pharos."

"I am at your bidding, my Queen." Demetrius bowed once more and took his leave.

CHAPTER FIVE

ROMAN CHESS

T HE ROMAN CONSULS HAD decided that the Coruncanius brothers would serve as the envoys to Illyria and Queen Teuta. They met with the brothers in the consul chamber to prepare them for their mission. Fabius took charge.

"Firstly, you will convey to the Queen our greetings from Rome. At the same time, you must express our concerns about her pirate attacks on our ships and that this represents a real problem to the Roman Empire. You must also explain to her that you are there, sent on behalf of the Empire, to negotiate a peaceful coexistence."

The brothers understood their task yet asked many questions, wanting their meeting with the Queen to be as pleasant and quick as possible. The older brother wanted specifics that were hard to come by. "What is the Queen's state of mind, and what forces do they have in the area?"

Some consuls felt that sending messengers was a futile gesture and that they should attack as soon as possible. Still, cool heads prevailed.

Q UEEN TEUTA HAD DECIDED that the meeting would be held at her new stronghold since her strength would be most visible there. She had asked Demetrius, Prince Darsej, Rron, and her father to be present. As the Roman ship approached Sucuraj, they all stood nervously on the steps of the dock.

Two men in Roman legion robes and another two in consular garb stepped off the vessel—one younger with light brown, almost blonde hair, the other angular with short-cropped brown hair. Both took in their surroundings, then smiled diplomatically.

The elder Roman spoke first. "Queen Teuta, it is a pleasure to meet you. We are brothers Coruncanius and represent the Consul of Rome."

Teuta's red-and-black outfit displayed both her strength and style. "Welcome to Illyria, how may we be of assistance?" Her tone was cordial but with a touch of arrogance that did not go unnoticed by the Romans.

"We are here to talk about a peaceful coexistence between Illyria and the Roman Empire. We are concerned about the actions of your pirates. The sea is neutral territory; we all need it for our countries' well-being, and we cannot allow the robberies to continue." The elder brother seemed to be the spokesman.

Teuta smiled. "I am grateful for the effort you made to visit me and my compatriots. Give my respects to the consuls. I do want to make it clear that according to Illyrian law, piracy is considered to be in the same category as fishing. It is a lawful enterprise that my government has no intention of stopping."

The brothers were taken aback. "Perhaps we can come to another sort of agreement, where your 'fishing men' decide to go after other prey and leave Roman ships alone," the elder consul suggested.

But the idea did not sit well with Teuta. "It would not be my place to tell citizens that such a lawful enterprise has certain restrictions. Perhaps it is best that you keep your ships out of Illyrian-controlled waters."

The younger Coruncanius shook his head in disbelief while the elder calmed him.

"We only have a desire to live peacefully and save your men from going to battle and certain *destruction*," the young statesman replied, emphasizing the word "destruction."

Teuta was fast losing her patience. These men came here expecting her to cower and submit, neither of which she would do. Putting aside her feelings for the moment, she offered hospitality to show that Illyrians were just as civilized as the Romans.

"Perhaps you can stay for dinner—try our cuisine and drink our wine." The generous words did not match her bitter tone.

"We are thankful for your offer, but that is not possible, Your Grace. We must get back to Rome immediately."

The elder consul bowed deeply, but his rejection of the Queen's invitation was an act of disrespect that rippled throughout the room. A low murmur among the generals and others in attendance raised the tension as the younger consul picked up where his brother left off.

"Our fellow consuls will be eager to hear your response and the way in which it was conveyed." It seemed Coruncanius junior could not restrain himself.

Teuta's face grew white and her jaw clenched. Demetrius stepped forward to try to calm the mood. "It would be wise, my young Roman friend, to accept our hospitality and discuss the matter over food and wine. Then we can accurately portray our concerns."

The older Coruncanius nodded in agreement, but his young brother laughed.

"What makes you think we would ever share a meal with pirates and outlaws?"

Teuta had had enough. Without a blink, she instinctively reached for her bow, seated the arrow, and shot the younger man in the eye as everyone looked on in disbelief. The Roman consul and guards were immediately surrounded by Teuta's men and forced to their knees. Teuta towered over them.

Shaken by the cold-blooded murder of his brother, Coruncanius senior exclaimed, "You have sealed your fate, Queen Teuta. Rome does not give pause when threatened in this manner."

Still looking down upon the Romans, Teuta motioned to her men. They drew their swords.

"I am Teuta, Queen of Illyria. I do not fear any man or any Kingdom. You came here under guise of negotiations and yet you dictate demands. I trust you will convey my message back to your leaders." She raised her hand, and the Illyrian soldiers removed the heads of all the Romans save the elder Coruncanius. Horrified at the massacre he had just witnessed, Coruncanius shook with fear.

"I will have the heads of your men put in a case, and you can take them back to your consuls. Tell them to leave Illyria alone,"

Teuta stated without fanfare, then turned and walked away. Silence fell upon the room, broken only by gasps and a few tears.

Demetrius and Rron caught up with Teuta after recovering from their initial shock.

"My Queen, please stop for a minute." Demetrius was tense and out of breath. "You are aware that your actions could very well lead to war with the Roman Empire?"

Teuta stopped and turned. "My dear cousin, you know as well as I that strength and ruthlessness are all these people know. We cannot appear weak."

"Yes, but…."

"Besides, they have no ships left. After our raids, it will take them years to rebuild, while we are prepared now. This time, we will not wait for them to attack us; we will be the aggressor while they are weak. Illyria will rule their own backyard." She turned and continued walking at a quick pace.

Demetrius directed Rron to return to his chambers, explaining that he needed to speak with the Queen. Rron objected, not wanting to be left alone.

Demetrius did not waver. "You can go back to Prince Darsej then until I am done."

Rron left reluctantly, thinking he would miss out on an important lesson. Demetrius ran to catch up with Teuta.

"My Queen, please, I have a private matter I must discuss."

Teuta stopped just outside her chamber doors, looked at Demetrius, and ushered him in.

"I understand your objection to my order, and I know I should take your counsel on such matters…."

Demetrius raised his hand to stop her from continuing. "I must admit I did not agree with your actions. You have put us all at risk; there will likely be retaliation, and it will be harsh on all the citizens of Illyria. I saw a side of you just now that I have never seen before. While this may not be the perfect time to bring up a personal matter...."

Queen Teuta blinked and sat on a nearby settee as he continued.

"Following Agron's death, I wanted to tell you but I could not find the courage. Tonight, seeing you like this, I am aware that I must say something before I find myself flung into another battle or stationed in a far-off land."

"This sounds dire, my dear Demetrius. I would have you tell me the truth."

"I am in love with you," Demetrius blurted out, louder than he had intended. He continued with a softer tone. "My love for you hurts my chest, my body, my soul. There is not a minute I do not think of you." He shivered with emotion.

Queen Teuta looked at him askance, not expecting such a confession and quite bewildered. He was right. The timing of this admission was odd; she had not had a chance to sufficiently calm herself from the day's turmoil. She blinked and remained silent for many moments, then stood and went to him, taking his hands in hers.

"My dear Demetrius, my general, my protector, my *cousin*. You serve Illyria with much passion and devotion." She emphasized "cousin" and squeezed his large calloused fingers. "As much as I am flattered and challenged by your emotions, I have taken an oath to myself that there will be no other man's hand on my body, or lips on my lips. King Agron's love and touch are still with me, in me, around me. I survive each day letting his spirit guide me. I gave my Besa to fight for Illyria until my last breath, and that is what I must do."

Demetrius was silent for a moment. "We share our Besa for Illyria, but is it right that we remain alone? Let me love you. There is no man who could love you more. King Agron would not mind were he able to speak from beyond the grave."

"Demetrius, I love you as a cousin and nothing more. Try to sleep, and tomorrow we will say nothing of this. You will find your love, your true love. I know you will."

She touched his cheek and he grabbed for her hand, but she pulled away. "It is time for my rest. Dora will be here in a moment. Go, sleep. You will see things clearly at daylight."

Demetrius left her chambers in so much pain he was not sure he could endure it.

QUEEN TEUTA WASTED NO time in making good on her promise to take the fight to the Romans. She ordered the siege of Issa and sent Demetrius to Corcyra to lead her forces there. Demetrius had hoped Teuta would see clear to have him oversee the siege while she was busy invading, but that seemed unlikely. He felt the Queen was punishing him for his admission of love and couldn't get the thought out of his mind, even though he loved her still.

The Romans received the heads of their ambassadors and called a meeting to discuss their actions against such a flagrant assault on their Empire.

Fabius was as furious as anyone had ever seen him. No object or person was safe in his path. "That evil witch, she cannot be allowed to continue her assault. We need to crush her, crush her armies and subdue all Illyrians to the will of Rome."

Many consuls nodded, but Postumius pondered the situation, chin in fist. "We need to be smarter than her because she is clever. We need to find an ally—someone she trusts—and turn him to our side. He will be our key to conquering Teuta."

"Yes, yes, and promise him the throne. We would then have all of Illyria and their armies at our disposal," the others chimed in.

Ecstatic at the reception his proposal received, Consul Postumius warned, "But we have to play the game carefully."

Fabius liked the idea and volunteered to pose as an Illyrian to gather information and find the right person to turn to their side. "She must pay for her actions. The day she murdered our ambassadors was the day she was doomed. Killing her will give me great pleasure."

CHAPTER SIX

LOVE HEALS
AND HURTS

THE ROMANS CAME UP with a plan to infiltrate the Illyrians, to gather information, and seek a way of subduing them. Fabius and his guards dressed as poor Illyrian peasants with arrows and many swords hidden among their provisions. Their plan was to embark from the ancient city of Jader, close to Pharos. It would be from Pharos that they would insinuate themselves into the Illyrian population.

Arriving in common fishing boats, the Roman spies stepped onto the shores of Pharos. Fabius muttered under his breath, "One step closer to your head, Teuta."

The band of Romans found lodging and ordered food and wine. Immediately, they spread out among the houses and squares, listening, asking questions.

Norik sat on the large cushions that had once been used by Agron, among a room full of memories in a Castle now void of energy and life. He burned incense and drank wine almost to the point of inebriation, just comfortable enough to be relaxed but alert enough to answer any calls. He remained under the employ of Arion and the former Queen but was far removed from the actual ruling of the Kingdom. His memories kept him as sane as he could be under the circumstances.

"Still missing your King Agron?" Arion startled him.

"Every day. Life seemed to lose meaning when he died. Now my days are long and nights even longer." Norik took a sip and offered Arion a seat.

Arion took his place across from Norik. "Things have definitely changed around here. All we can do is remember and celebrate the life that he led, the Kingdom he forged. But you, my friend, you have to move on. Get married, have a family, bring new meaning to your life, and make new memories."

Norik shook his head.

Arion persisted. "I am meeting Bersant for a walk around the city and the market. Join us. It isn't good to sit here all day alone; you need company." Arion put his hand on Norik's shoulder for encouragement.

"Bersant is not the company I prefer, thank you." Norik replied.

Arion shook his head. "Are you still at it, after all these years? I don't understand the feud between you two. What if I commanded you to accompany me?"

"I would have to comply as a loyal servant, but I do not need to like it."

Bersant was already in the market when Arion greeted him. "Good morning, Master Bersant. How are you?" Arion bowed slightly while Norik paid attention to some fruit.

"Well, my friend, it is a beautiful day, is it not?" Bersant motioned for Arion to sit, ignoring Norik. "May I offer you some refreshment?"

He poured water for Arion. "I am glad you stopped by today. I have had some disturbing dreams. Blood, dead horses, swords, more blood. They have been waking me up in the early hours of the morning. I am afraid they are bad omens."

"What do you think they mean?" Arion took a drink.

"I believe that Queen Teuta is doing a remarkable job with her strategy and leading her army. I hear that her town and Castle are nearly complete, and plans for more buildings are being drawn up."

"And?" Arion was getting impatient.

Bersant nodded. "It has been a while since the incident with the Roman ambassadors, and yet we have heard nothing. Romans are most dangerous when silent. I fear they are planning something." He began pacing nervously. "We should pay a visit to Queen Teuta and discuss the circumstances."

"Circumstances?" Norik spoke up for the first time. "Don't you think Queen Teuta knows what the result of her actions will be? What new information can you bring her that is not just conjecture or dreams of bloody battles? All battles are bloody."

Bersant was displeased with comments on policies he deemed to be above Norik's station. "You are the stable boy, the waiter, a fish monger's son. What would you know about such matters?"

"There is nothing in this Kingdom, in this Castle, that I have not witnessed," Norik rebutted his superior, "and I can see clearly how you intend to use this 'crisis' toward your own end rather than in support of the Realm."

"I will have you hold your tongue!" Bersant slammed his fist on the table.

"Or what? I am not afraid of you, old man. For all your posturing and conniving, what have you gained? If you are going to Queen Teuta, I intend to accompany you," Norik stated resolutely.

"No, under no circumstances will you accompany me!" Bersant responded with a resounding no.

Arion chimed in apologetically. "If you go, Norik, who will stay and look after Queen Apollonia? There is no one I trust more than you. And it is just as important that we know Epidamnus is in good hands."

Norik saw no argument to counter Arion's plea. "I will do as you command," he acquiesced.

"We leave tomorrow," Bersant informed them.

Arion looked at Bersant. Norik had made him think.

APOLLONIA WAS NOT PLEASED. She begged Arion to take her with him, but he flatly refused.

"It's not good timing. Next time, my love. I promise. We will only be a few days."

"I don't understand why all of a sudden you have to leave. Is there something you are hiding from me?" She came up to Arion, touching his chest. "Is Rron all right?"

"Yes, he is fine. We just decided it was good timing and necessary at the moment." He gathered his things, and Apollonia choked back her sobs.

"Stay well," Arion said tenderly. "Norik will be here. Trust me, my love, I will be back very soon."

He hugged and kissed Apollonia, but it did not relieve the feeling of dread that had come over her. She watched as Arion, Bersant, and their guards rode away from the Castle. She felt helpless and utterly alone.

QUEEN TEUTA'S NEW FLAGSHIP, the Liburnia, had just been completed, and revelry and excitement greeted Arion and Bersant as they arrived at Fort Agron. The Queen stood on the massive deck of the ship and toasted all her boat smiths and workers with full wine cups and a feast of lamb, goat, fish, and fruit from the Liburnian tribe, the inspiration for her prized warship.

After Teuta's speech and rousing applause from her subjects, she returned to her quarters to find Arion and Bersant waiting for her there. Poor Dora had been overwhelmed by the general and high counselor's adamancy about seeing the Queen.

"Gentlemen, this is a surprise. What brings you here? Are there problems in Epidamnus?" She motioned for the men to be seated as Dora came to get her staff and crown.

"We needed to pay you a visit," Bersant said before Arion could get a word out. "There is an urgent matter that needs your attention."

"Is it so urgent that we must interrupt the festivities? My people have worked hard for this, and I will not deny them the enjoyment." Her gaze bored into Bersant, blaming him for the turn of mood.

Arion spoke up, preempting Bersant. "We believe that the Romans are prepared to strike, and we would like to meet with the generals to discuss strategy."

"Where did you get this information?"

"A reliable source," Arion replied.

"I have had many spies keep a close watch on the Romans and have heard nothing of this." Teuta was skeptical.

Arion looked at Bersant, who suddenly grew silent, perhaps realizing that their trip had been a mistake. Bersant's standing with the new Queen was on shaky ground, and although he was considered the Chief Consul, Teuta was not sure of his wisdom. Still, they were there, and his feelings about Rome were strong.

Arion had no choice but to back Bersant or betray his trust. "If we could just meet with you and the generals…. It is important to look at all information that could threaten Illyria."

"Alright, you will have your meeting tomorrow morning." Teuta turned to Dora. "Please send for General Gentius and tell him to meet me here immediately." Dora bowed and hurried out of the chambers.

Gentius was the youngest of her Pirate Generals and loyal to a fault. Teuta asked him to gather the generals, including Demetrius, Prince Darsej, and several other key advisors for the meeting. Once that was done, she saw to it that Arion and Bersant were shown to adequate quarters, then summoned an amphora of red wine and a bath to be drawn for herself.

Finally alone, Teuta felt the ocean breeze lilt through the window and over her body like Agron's breath. In the silence of the bath with the candles burning, she let go and cried, suddenly overcome by the magnitude of her responsibilities. She called out to Agron to help her through the night and guide her into the morning.

FABIUS AND HIS MEN had been in Pharos for many days mingling with the people in the market, acquiring information, and discovering secrets that could suit their plan well. It seemed that Demetrius—the ruler of Pharos and one of Teuta's prime generals—was disappointed in the treatment he was receiving from the Queen. Still, he was one of King Agron's childhood friends, Teuta's cousin, and loyal to Illyria. It seemed an impossible task to even get near him.

The evening was upon them, and Giannius, a tall, thin, and agile consul offered Fabius a glass of wine, interrupting his deep thoughts. Fabius had been talking to himself but turned his thoughts outward when Giannius handed him the wine.

"Demetrius is the only person around Queen Teuta with the information we need. He has no wife, no children, no family.... He doesn't even have an ambition to become King. How are we supposed to find the leverage we need? There must be a weak point." Giannius shook his head, puzzled. "There has to be something...a lover, friends…give me permission, and I will find out about his private life."

Just then a guard ran up to the two men, out of breath. Between gasps he uttered, "There is a celebration…. Queen Teuta has invited all the workers and artists to celebrate the completion of their warships. All the important people are attending."

Fabius brightened. "A stroke of luck, we must leave immediately."

THE MUSIC, WINE, WOMEN, and singing were all over by the time Fabius and his men arrived. Drunks and beggars were all that remained. The ships, swaying gently at their moorings, were the biggest Fabius had ever seen.

He grabbed a drunk walking by. "What is the name of this ship?"

"The Liburn…Liburni…Liburnia." The drunk stuttered and stumbled on his way.

In the distance, they could see a group of men standing near the ship, some dressed as workers and a few in military garb. Fabius decided to approach them.

"Good evening, fellow Illyrians." He pretended to be happy with drink. The men turned to him with suspicion.

"Isn't she magnificent?" Fabius pointed to the Liburnia.

The men seemed to relax a little. "It ought to be; we worked for almost a year building it. Not even the Roman Empire possesses a ship like this," crowed a bearded, long-haired artisan with rough hands.

"Haven't we seized all their ships?" Fabius joked.

The worker laughed. "They will need years to build new ones, and by then we will rule the sea."

"I have heard much about General Demetrius," Fabius commented. "He is a legend of our tribe. Have you met him?"

"I have seen him. In fact, there he is, standing with his soldiers and advisor Master Bersant. They are preparing for the launching of the ship tomorrow." The worker pointed to Demetrius dressed in plain armor but towering over his men.

"He looks like an impressive man," Fabius observed. "A man like that must have a beautiful wife and handsome children."

"He has never married; the rumor is that he is in love with Queen Teuta." The worker leaned in as he whispered the gossip to these complete strangers.

"But I thought he was King Agron's best friend and the Queen's cousin?"

"Exactly. Those are most likely the reasons she turned him away." The worker winked. "Also, she sent him on a mission but damaged his pride by fighting the battle without him."

"I would be upset if I were in his place. Perhaps you could introduce me to him?"

"I have no personal communication with the general. I would be a stranger to him." The worker lost interest in the conversation and started walking away.

"Perhaps you could tell me where he lives at least, and we can make our own introductions. It would be a shame to come all this way and not pay homage to the great Demetrius."

"Everyone knows where he lives. It is the only stone house on the bay. He is particular about the view, wanting to see all that come and go from the harbor."

One of Fabius' guards approached the worker from behind, his knife drawn, ready to eliminate him, but Fabius motioned the guard away. No sense in leaving a body for people to ask questions about.

T HE ROMANS APPROACHED DEMETRIUS' house with caution since a legion of guards surrounded it and they weren't even sure he was home at the moment. Luck was with them. At that moment, Demetrius approached with Bersant and two more guards. He stopped at his doorway and sent the guards away. Fabius told his men to stay back, while Giannius warned Fabius that Demetrius was not alone. First putting his fingers to Giannius' lips to silence him, Fabius approached the house alone. He knocked on the door.

"Who is it?" Demetrius demanded.

"A friend from Rome," Fabius ventured, unsure how Demetrius would respond. A tense silence ensued. Fabius envisioned Demetrius calling his guards back. A few moments later, the door opened.

Demetrius was obviously in a foul mood. "Who are you?"

Fabius revealed his Roman dress under the villager rags. Demetrius immediately went for his sword, but Bersant calmed him.

"I know this man, my Lord; he has a proposal that I think you will want to listen to."

"He is a Roman spy who dares enter my home," Demetrius growled.

Bersant continued, attempting to dissipate Demetrius's anger. "These are honorable men. I know you are dedicated to Illyria. That is why they have come."

"They are our enemy, and it seems so are you." Demetrius threatened Bersant with his sword.

Bersant parried with a challenge. "You are a smart man, my Lord. You know that Illyria cannot defeat the Romans, but what if we could save Illyria through an alliance rather than the Kingdom being humiliated and divided?"

Demetrius wavered, hearing logic in the proposal.

Fabius presented him a document.

"What does it hurt to take a look at their proposal? Then you can decide and call your guards or not," Bersant rasped through a dry throat.

Demetrius thought for a moment, then took the parchment from Fabius. He read that it was signed by the consuls and gave Fabius power to speak on their behalf.

"I come in peace," Fabius insisted. "I am here to talk about our concerns regarding Queen Teuta."

Demetrius glanced between the letter and Fabius with skepticism.

"What is it you want from me? I am not a friend of Rome and have sworn my Besa to Illyria." He handed the letter back to Fabius, who registered his hesitation.

"As Bersant has said, you would be saving Illyria. The only other option is for Rome to invade and totally obliterate your Kingdom. We restrained ourselves in our initial dealings with the new Queen. Think of it…we sent diplomatic envoys whose heads were sent back in a bag. Did you not think that Rome would react strongly to such an insult?"

Demetrius listened and understood their proposal. They wanted him to defect, to hand over his army and lands to the Romans in exchange…. For what? was the only question.

As if reading Demetrius's mind, Fabius laid out their proposal. Demetrius would get to rule Pharos, and after the Queen had been subdued, he would rule all Illyria. Although it wasn't his desire to become King, Demetrius saw the proposal as an opportunity to purge his feelings of betrayal and rejection. Teuta had been clear that there was no other option for Demetrius besides being her servant for the rest of his life, and that was not acceptable to him. As for Bersant, Demetrius knew what the advisor wanted…the same things he had always craved: influence and power. While Demetrius knew that Bersant's motives were selfish, he had seen the threat to Illyria clearly. For that, Demetrius was almost ready to forgive him for his treason, the treason he himself was contemplating.

Bersant, on the other hand, was counting on Demetrius's actions, for his endgame was far more complex than mere treason.

CHAPTER SEVEN

TRUST

ALL THE GENERALS, ADVISORS, and royals were gathering for the meeting with Queen Teuta. Gentius was in charge of the greetings and making sure everyone attended. Servants brought in wine, olives, and water.

Meanwhile, Teuta was meeting alone with Bersant before she was to bring the meeting to order. "I understand your concerns, Master Bersant," Teuta conceded after listening to his theories. "But I decide how I will rule. I understand that the Roman silence concerns you, and I am willing to bring that point up at the counsel along with my plans. Is there anything else?"

Bersant anticipated the Queen's response and had something else up his sleeve.

"Yes, in fact there is, my Queen." Teuta bristled a bit but listened nonetheless. "I noticed Demetrius acting out of sorts at the celebration last night. I have never seen him so sullen at a party before. He behaved oddly when near you, and I could not tell if it was out of love or hate."

"Master Bersant, my personal life should not be of concern to you. How someone acts around me is not my worry. How they act *for* me is." She rose from her chair.

"My point, Your Majesty, is that if a personal matter exists between you and Demetrius, it could have repercussions for the Kingdom. That is my concern."

Teuta gathered herself, then looked directly at Bersant, telling him with her icy stare that he had better watch his step. "I have known Demetrius all my life. I have confidence in his abilities as a commander and a loyal Illyrian. That is all there is to say." She made her way past Bersant and headed to the meeting chamber.

Everyone stood as Queen Teuta entered the chamber, their right hands on their hearts as was the Illyrian tradition. Bersant followed quietly a distance behind, attuned to the faces of all in attendance. He noticed that Demetrius was distracted and was not holding his right hand over his heart.

After everyone settled in, Teuta began. She congratulated those who had just returned from successful campaigns, then applauded those responsible for finishing her fleet of ships, and so forth and so on, until finally she paused.

"I have a plan I want to discuss with you."

A low mumble rumbled among the attendees. Teuta motioned one of the servants to bring out a large map and suggested everyone to gather around.

"I believe we should attack the Romans at their border near Pola, using the local tribes to reinforce our soldiers. We have ten thousand soldiers and one hundred twenty ships ready and can make significant headway before having to resupply."

Her plan drew much discussion, and the people spent hours suggesting revisions, alternate approaches, and timing. Demetrius argued that the timeline for the attack should be shortened from thirty days to ten since the new Liburnian ships would serve as more powerful weapons. Teuta liked his suggestion and agreed.

The longer the evening went and the more Bersant observed Demetrius, the more wary he became. Finally, he summoned Arion and Gentius to his quarters and shared with them his concerns.

"I have known Demetrius since he was a child, and I have never seen him act this way. Arion, stay close to Queen Teuta and Gentius. I will go back to Epidamnus alone. Someone needs to keep an eye on Demetrius but with caution. I will be the first watch, as I will be leaving early in the morning."

Arion accepted Bersant's request. It would also give him a chance to see Rron and to assure Apollonia of his own health and well-being.

Bersant left as quickly as he could and turned down the street to Demetrius's house.

F ABIUS AND THE OTHER Romans were waiting for Demetrius when he returned from the meeting. He explained how he moved the invasion schedule to within 10 days and that it would make the Illyrians less cautious. Still, he was not comfortable with the plan.

There was something about Fabius and his attitude that sent his stomach churning, or perhaps it was the information that the Romans gave him; either way his unease was a sure sign to exert caution. He must put all his feelings aside for the good of his beloved land, most importantly, the still fresh feelings of both love and rejection.

The Romans told Demetrius that they had twenty thousand soldiers and two hundred ships ready to attack in nine days. Illyria had a little more than half those numbers; they would be overwhelmed, and now with his added forces, there was no chance that the Kingdom would stand with Teuta as Queen.

After the Romans left Demetrius, they circled back to an alley near the shipwright's station. They waited for a few minutes until a hooded figure approached. Fabius met with the man, passing him some coins.

"You have been a valuable asset," Fabius murmured. "We are thankful. It seems the Queen has made some unhappy counselors."

Fabius and his men moved off as Bersant removed his hood and departed in the opposite direction.

Demetrius spent a fitful night questioning his planned betrayal. He knew his decision wasn't just about Illyria or the promise of power. It was a choice wrapped up in his fated love for Teuta and saving her from herself since, after much bargaining, the Romans had agreed to let her live out her life in peace.

ARION AND GENTIUS WERE preparing their soldiers for war. Before Bersant departed for his journey, he pulled them aside to suggest that one of them invite Demetrius for some revelry while the other search his house for signs of betrayal. He warned them not to bother Teuta with the plan, that she had enough to keep her occupied...that any threat to her Kingdom would be dealt with out of hand.

During Bersant's last audience with Queen Teuta, he had made a point of praising her bravery and wisdom, commending her for keeping all the Illyrian tribes together. He had also declared it an honor to be serving her. She had given him a nod and a quick smile, still not convinced of his sincerity or his loyalty. He had felt her skepticism but had known that the events of the coming days would change the fate of everyone, and he was sure to be there to pick up the pieces.

ARION MET UP WITH Demetrius on the training field. They sparred for a few rounds before taking a break to get out of the scorching sun. Though there was a breeze blowing across Pharos, it brought little relief. The two men drank deeply from the water buckets and laughed at the sight of each other drenched in sweat.

"There is no better feeling then after a good fight," Arion ventured. Demetrius agreed. "I would like to ask you a favor," Arion continued.

"A favor?"

"Yes. As you know, I have traveled many days to get here. Now, because of training, I have neglected to enjoy my stay in your land. And since you are well acquainted with the best places for wine and women, I am hoping you can show me around to drink together and enjoy entertainment with me and Gentius."

Demetrius hesitated. He was not used to drinking and was very selective in his women. He felt a certain obligation, however, to provide hospitality, and the gesture would steer suspicion away from him.

"I would be pleased to share a drink with you, although I do have to retire early."

"As do we all." Arion slapped Demetrius on the back. "I will meet you at the Castle at dusk. I need a long bath." He smiled.

QUEEN TEUTA HAD BEEN training with her pirates and the physical exertion had worn her out. She looked forward to a bath and some dinner. She summoned Dora and instructed her which outfit she would like to wear for the evening. Dora bounced in full of energy, hardly able to contain her excitement.

"Dora, my goodness, what is it? You look like you are ready to burst."

"My Queen, it is good news. The guard you sent to look for Rron's Dorotea has been successful! Tomorrow, he will bring her to Fort Agron and reunite her with the Prince."

Teuta smiled and hugged Dora. Although happy for Rron and his love, the news made her feel all that more alone without Agron. She would give them her blessings and support their wishes, and even conceal the event from Apollonia if need be, but she was also saddened by it.

Dorotea had grown into a beautiful young woman with blonde hair and blue eyes. Rron, however, still looked thirteen, but his love for her was even more powerful than before. Their union brightened the surroundings amid the dark forebodings of war that Illyria was facing. The citizens used the couple's reunion as a celebration to keep their minds off the coming battles.

Rron and Arion continued their lessons, but Arion made it clear that Rron was never to go into battle—that he was too valuable as the heir to the throne to risk his life. While Rron reluctantly accepted the fact that he might never see battle in the coming war, he was still his father's son, with the same drive and intensity he had used in helping to build the Castle and fleet. The one thing that softened his intensity was his reunion with Dorotea. Having someone he cared about within Fort Agron made him willing to ensure the city's defense.

ARION MET UP WITH Gentius at the marketplace in order to hear what he had found after searching Demetrius's home. When Gentius informed him that there seemed to be nothing of interest, Arion would not believe it.

"I don't think you looked hard enough," he declared.

"If I hadn't left when I did, he would have found me going through his things! You were supposed to keep him occupied longer," Gentius complained vigorously.

"We will have another chance tonight when I meet him for celebrations. You can go back and look harder this time."

"But he is expecting me to join the both of you. I had to make up a story as to why I was at the docks and near his house, so I told him I was bringing the invitation."

Arion looked hard at Gentius. "We will have to make an excuse for your absence."

ARION HAD TOLD DEMETRIUS to meet him in the market. He had been waiting for over an hour, while peasants were continually coming up to him with goods to buy, most of which, he surmised, were stolen or rotting. Even in this new and thriving city, poverty seemed to sprout from nothing and blossom as it did throughout the Illyrian Kingdom.

Demetrius finally arrived with a guard in tow. Arion was surprised to say the least.

Demetrius greeted them. "Good evening,"

"Good evening, General Demetrius. I have experienced your fighting skills first hand and believe a guard is not necessary for an evening of rousing fun and drink."

"This is Benedictus, my friend and brother-in-arms for many campaigns. He needed some time to relax, and I thought what better than to bring him along. After all, with Gentius I would become an awkward third party. Where is Gentius by the way?" Demetrius looked around.

"He has been delayed and will probably meet up with us later. Your friend is welcome, although unexpected." Arion was trying not to convey his concern; confronting Demetrius with whatever Gentius found could be a problem now.

As they made their way to the marketplace, Demetrius's guard kept a watchful eye on Arion, and it made him uneasy.

"This is the best place I know," Demetrius said as he stopped in front of a pair of wooden doors with dirty red curtains hanging in front. He opened the door and invited Arion to join him.

Demetrius's considerable knowledge of the city and its surroundings was presenting an ever-greater concern to Arion.

GENTIUS RETURNED TO DEMETRIUS'S house and searched all the rooms, still to no avail. He sat on one of the stout benches near the fireplace, frustrated and ready to leave empty-handed when he noticed something unusual. One of the hearthstones had obviously been removed and replaced. Pulling on the rock, he attempted to move it and was surprised at the ease with which it came loose. In a space behind it, he discovered a parchment with Roman lettering and signatures that he could not read but was nevertheless convinced that it was an important and damning document. He rolled it up and stuffed it into his shirt.

Arion was keeping Demetrius and Benedictus entertained as best he could, although he always ended up drinking more than them and was getting tipsy.

"Now let's get some beautiful girls to feed us grapes, kiss our lips, and caress our skins."

"I want to thank you for your invitation and company," Demetrius replied, "but I am tired and feel a little ill." He gently pushed away an advancing girl dressed in bright colors and with bare bosoms.

Gentius appeared in the doorway looking for Arion. Taking the opportunity to stall Demetrius, Arion greeted Gentius loudly. "Over here, my good general, I am glad you could join us."

Gentius made his way over to Arion, surprised by the presence of Benedictus.

"You must stay and have a drink with your comrade," Arion implored Demetrius as he welcomed Gentius to their table.

"May I have a word with you?" Gentius asked Arion without even acknowledging his two comrades-in-arms. Demetrius looked suspiciously at Gentius.

Arion tried to act the jovial host and keep suspicion at bay. "Have a drink first, my friend, and greet your fellow soldiers." Gentius grabbed a cup, saluted the men, and drank it dry. Wiping his mouth, he repeated that he needed to talk with Arion immediately—that it was a matter of great importance.

"You will excuse us for a moment. It seems Gentius will not be cheered." Arion bowed to Demetrius.

Retreating to a corner of the room, Arion expressed his displeasure. "What is it? You must be out of your mind."

Gentius took the scroll from his shirt and showed it to Arion. "I found this. It looked suspicious, but I cannot read. If it is nothing of importance, then I need to put it back in its place. If it is something of value, do we not need to confront Demetrius?"

Arion read the letter and turned pale. "We can't confront him here. He will know that we searched his house and had suspicions. At the very least, he could escape with his man, Benedictus, and at the worst, he could murder us and claim we had violated his private person. We need to speak with Queen Teuta."

Returning to the table, Arion was dismissive when asked about Gentius' news.

"It is a personal matter, nothing to be alarmed about. Please, let's just have a good time." He raised his cup, and the others followed suit.

It appeared to Arion that Bersant was right to keep an eye on Demetrius but was not forthcoming in what to do if a problem arose. Bersant had gone, leaving it up to Arion to decide a course of action. The situation gave him a great opportunity to curry favor with the Queen and other royals, including Rron. Yet he was still torn about telling Queen Teuta too soon. Bringing news of a problem is not as good as having already solved it.

CHAPTER EIGHT

THE TRAITOR

ARION PACED HIS QUARTERS, trying to get some clarity. He held the letter, reading it again and again. No doubt the content was treasonous, yet he had no information on whether or not Demetrius was planning to act on the conditions mentioned within. If Demetrius was planning to bring the Romans' plans to Teuta's attention, he would surely need the letter as proof, thereby securing his place higher in the military command, even as far as Regent. It's what Arion would do in his place, and that would reveal that they had taken the letter from Demetrius's house—proof of their treason in Teuta's eyes. Then again, if Demetrius was a traitor, it should be revealed sooner rather than later.

Arion wished Bersant was present; he would know what to do. Arion's head hurt from thinking. He sent for Gentius. Perhaps between the two of them, they could come up with a plan.

"We should wait and see if he notices it is gone," Gentius proposed.

"How are we going to do that? We would have to watch him every hour of every day he is at home." Arion shook his head, dismissing the suggestion.

"We could say that some of our pirates got out of control and robbed some of the portside houses and you found the letter among the things that were taken." *Another brilliant idea*, Arion groaned to himself.

"Did you take anything else from his house?"

"No, I made sure everything was where it was supposed to be."

"Then that obviously won't work." Arion was getting frustrated. Perhaps it wasn't a good idea to involve Gentius in the problem.

"Perhaps I could go back, take a few things and make it look like a robbery. Then it would work," Gentius offered.

"That might work. I could invite him for a sparring session while you go into his house. But you will have to be quick. Sparring with Demetrius is tiring."

"Yes, just let me know when."

"Today, this evening, when it's cooled down." Arion bit his lip. This might work.

"Make sure you leave the loosened brick out of the fireplace so he knows it was taken."

"OK. I will wait for Demetrius to leave with you." Gentius attempted to hide his nervousness. He really didn't want to go back to Demetrius's house. Returning to the scene of mischief was tempting fate, yet this matter was of grave importance to the Kingdom.

Over an hour passed before Gentius saw Arion enter Demetri-us's house, and another half an hour before the two men exited and headed for the training grounds. He saw them laughing, throwing jabs at each other to test their reflexes. Once they were out of sight, Gentius entered the house. He wasn't sure what to do exactly since he had never been a burglar, but he decided to take what he thought was valuable and knock over chairs, chests, and sculptures in the process to make it look like drunken sailors had been involved in the theft. He filled up a sack he had brought with him and was gone within ten minutes.

Gentius stayed close by, curious about Demetrius's reaction to the theft and ransacking of his house.

When Demetrius returned, without Arion, he entered his house but did not leave as Gentius thought he would. After waiting a couple of hours, Gentius returned to his own house and waited for the dawn.

T HE NEXT MORNING, ARION sent guards to fetch Demetrius, who was not happy, first because of the break-in to his house and second because it was early in the morning. He had been looking forward to a day of rest after a hard training session the previous evening.

Flanked by guards and suspicious of the meeting, Demetrius entered the hall. Arion and Gentius stood conversing and turned to him with welcoming gestures.

"My dear Demetrius," Arion cooed. "It has come to my attention that you have been wronged. Your home was broken into and valuables stolen."

"Yes, that is true. Oddly enough, the break-in happened while we were sparring on the training field," Demetrius responded.

"You will be happy to know that we have apprehended the offenders and recovered your property." Arion and Gentius smiled. Arion motioned to a nearby guard who held a large sack. The guard came over to Demetrius and emptied it at his feet. Candleholders, cups, silverware came tumbling out onto the floor.

Demetrius took stock of the possessions. "Everything seems to be here," he noted.

The guard began putting the items back in the bag.

"Excellent," Arion declared.

"Thank you for resolving this crime so quickly." Demetrius picked up the sack and bowed to Arion and Gentius.

"There is one thing." Arion was coy.

Demetrius hesitated, suspicious that the real intent of the meeting was about to be revealed.

"We found this among the items stolen." Gentius handed Arion the letter, who held it up for Demetrius to see. Arion and Gentius looked at him expectantly. Demetrius did not flinch. He knew it was a trap, and he was not going to play into their hands.

"What is that?"

"You know what it is. It was found in your...among your other stolen possessions." Arion thrust the letter in Demetrius's direction.

"I'm sorry. I do not know what that is. I have never seen it before." They wanted to play? He was glad to oblige.

"How would you not know something that was in your keeping?" Arion was taken off guard.

"Yes, it was among your things." Gentius remarked while Arion gave him a withering stare. "It was in the sack with the other items," he tried to explain.

"And yet still I have no knowledge of the document. What is it?"

"It is a treasonous letter from Rome," Gentius answered.

"Why in the name of the Gods would I have a treasonous letter?" The question took both Arion and Gentius by surprise.

"It is proof that you have been conspiring with the enemy." Arion's tone was stern.

"I have told you, I have never seen that letter before. Perhaps whoever broke into my house had it with them when they pilfered my belongings." The ball was now in Demetrius's court. Arion and Gentius could not reveal that they had actually been the thieves.

"Let me talk to the culprits, and I will get the truth out of them." Demetrius challenged.

Arion hesitated. "They…have been dealt with."

"That is a shame. Perhaps now we will never get to the bottom of this. Perhaps we can bring this matter up with my *cousin* Queen Teuta and see what she has to say."

When Demetrius emphasized the word "cousin," Arion looked at Gentius. They had been outmaneuvered, and while they knew that Demetrius was guilty, they could not say anything without exposing themselves.

"Perhaps we shall," were Arion's only words.

"I take it I am free to leave?" Demetrius stood.

There was nothing for Arion to say. He nodded with a grimace. Demetrius picked up his items and left.

"What will we do now?" Gentius asked Arion.

"We will bring the issue up to the Queen and see what she has to say about it. Demetrius isn't as smart as he thinks he is. The Queen has final judgment; her word is all that matters."

T ROOPS AND SHIPS WERE on the move, pouring out of Fort Agron to their predetermined positions in preparation for Illyrians' campaign against the Romans. Information regarding Roman numbers and fleet was confirmed, and Queen Teuta wanted the element of surprise. Studying the map spread across the table in the middle of her anteroom, she went over and over the plan in her head. At first, she did not hear Dora announcing the presence of Arion and Gentius. When their presence finally registered with her, she rose.

"Gentlemen," she greeted them without formality. "Should you not be with your soldiers? We are about to embark on a very important mission."

"Yes, my Queen. However, we have an important matter to discuss, one that could be of grave importance to the campaign."

"I am listening."

Gentius handed the letter to Teuta. She looked first at him, then at the letter.

"What is this? It is in a Roman hand."

"Yes, Your Majesty."

"It was found in Demetrius' house hidden in his fireplace." Arion's voice cracked a little.

"Demetrius?" The Queen raised her eyebrows.

"Yes, my Queen. The letter is from the Roman Fabius, giving Demetrius title over Pharos and ultimately over Illyria if he defects to their cause."

"I don't believe it. I have known Demetrius all my life. He introduced me to King Agron. How could he betray the country he loves?" Teuta threw the letter back at Gentius. "Have you asked him about this?"

"Yes, Your Majesty. He claims to know nothing about it."

"And yet this was found in his house? By whom?"

Gentius stepped forward.

"By me, Your Grace."

"Then how could he deny this?"

Things got sticky for Arion and Gentius at this point. Arion made the first attempt at explaining. "In order to confront Demetrius with the proof without making him suspicious and leave the city, we told him that his house had been burgled and that the letter was among the items stolen."

"And he denied having seen it, accusing the thieves of taking it from another house?" Arion and Gentius nodded.

"You are better at leading your troops than being involved in espionage with someone like Demetrius. It is obvious that he is guilty of treason and should be imprisoned. I will give the order. You, General Arion and General Gentius, go to your men and follow your orders."

They both bowed and hurried out.

NORIK WATCHED AS BERSANT rode his horse into the Castle and was surprised that Arion was not with him. When Bersant drew near, Norik took the reins and helped him dismount.

"Thank you, Norik." It might have been the first time Bersant had actually said something amicable to his old adversary.

"Where is General Arion?"

"He stayed to help Queen Teuta in her campaign against the Romans. It appears that my information proved valuable after all." Bersant smirked. "Arion's presence is needed there now more than ever."

"Queen Apollonia will not be happy. And what of Rron?"

"He has worked hard and will remain with Queen Teuta at the new Castle until the battle is over. He reunited with his love Dorotea and is very happy."

Norik led Bersant's horse toward the stable.

"I shouldn't mention that to Queen Apollonia, since she sent Dorotea away," Norik warned.

"I am aware."

"So there is to be a new war?" Norik wanted all the information about what he was missing out on.

"Yes, it will be the biggest yet. Let the Gods be with us." Bersant tried to look concerned.

"Just what you wanted...a conflict to stick your nose in and further your ambitions," Norik scoffed.

Bersant laughed. "My dear Norik, I am too old to have ambitions."

"If only that were true." Norik closed the stable gate.

"Enough of this banter. Tell me, how is Queen Apollonia?"

"Worried for General Arion. She will be happy to hear all the news you can supply. I am afraid she is in love and has had many dark days and nights."

"Light and dark, sun and moon, black and white, these are the ways of our existence."

"Poetry in your old age?" Norik quipped.

"I am old, Norik, and so are you. We have been sparring with our words for many decades now, but I am growing tired. Where I used to be filled with ambition and plans for greatness, I realize that I have to settle for what I have accomplished."

"As painful as this is for me to admit," Norik responded, "you have given a few bits of wise counsel to King Agron and both Queens, Apollonia and Teuta."

"Ah, well, Queen Teuta has been cold toward my advice, and I am afraid her impetuousness and inexperience will not serve the greater good of Illyria."

Bersant's assessment shocked Norik. "But surely her desire is to follow the plans of her great love, King Agron, and improve the Kingdom?"

"There is a difference between desire and ability."

Norik shook his head. "She is revered far and wide for being a strong and decisive leader, a fierce warrior. Are you sure we are talking about the same Queen Teuta?"

"There are forces at work that do not bode well for her, and we must think more about our beloved Kingdom then the Queen."

"Are you talking about treason? What have you done? Is your wish to leave such a legacy behind that when your bones are dust and ash, that is all to be remembered of you? Do you realize you would be betraying your Besa to King Agron, Queen Teuta, and all of Illyria?"

"You are mistaken. I am not the guilty party. I'm just aware, like the birds sensing a change in the weather."

D EMETRIUS KNEW THAT HIS thin explanation about the Roman document to Arion and Gentius would not hold up under the more sophisticated and intelligent mind of his cousin. So he left in the dead of night, disappearing with his soldiers, blending into the stream of military spreading out across the land. The news of his betrayal surprised everyone. Rron and Prince Darsej were in shock. It came at a most sensitive time, only a few days before the planned attack, and now they could not count on Demetrius's forces. Everything had to change and a new plan be devised. The Illyrian spies confirmed that the Romans were approaching with two hundred new warships and twenty thousand soldiers from sea and land.

Their forces outnumbered, the Illyrians had to depend on being able to hold strategic locations, attacking with surprise and desisting from engaging in long battles they could not win. All the generals and consuls agreed that Illyria's most important asset and advantage was Queen Teuta. The Romans feared her and knew she was to be taken seriously, even if they win the war. As long as she was still free, there was hope for Illyria.

Her most trusted advisors and friends had convinced Queen Teuta to retreat to the Illyrian base in Scutari, which was surrounded by mountains and easily defended. Preparations for an extended stay were made and forty of the elite guards were to accompany her.

Teuta was naturally opposed to the idea. Every fiber of her being wanted to be in the midst of battle. She had been bred for it, the Gods had set her on the path of a warrior, and there was nothing she wouldn't do to stand with her men and die a glorious death if that is what the Gods willed. Retreating to the mountains was a cowardly thing to do, in her opinion, and yet she knew that the betrayal of Demetrius left her little choice.

"May all the Gods be with you," Queen Teuta saluted Arion, Gentius, and Rron.

"And the Gods be with you, my Queen. Stay well and do not look back; know that we will fight for Illyria until our last breath." Arion had his hand on his heart.

Gentius kneeled with his head bowed. He could not bring himself to look at Teuta for fear of losing control of his emotions.

But Teuta leaned down to him. "Gentius, take my sword. You made it for me. The crimson stone you put in it will be my eye blessing you in this great fight."

Gentius accepted the sword then returned to kneeling, his voice raspy. "Thank you, my Queen. Your spirit will be with us in battle, your heart the beating of the drums."

"Long live Queen Teuta," the cry rang out, over and over in the hazy morning air.

Just before the Queen departed, a peasant boy approached her. The guards intervened, but she motioned to let him pass. He presented a letter. She wasn't sure what to make of it but thanked the boy and gave him a coin. Unraveling the parchment, she gasped. It was in Demetrius's hand.

My Queen, I stopped living the day you refused my love. I have had many sleepless nights and anguished days. Yet know that despite your rejection, my love for you will never die. I have made an agreement with the Romans that will save your life, for surely you know that we cannot overcome their numbers on the ground or sea. Escape, be safe, and remember our better days on Pharos.

She reread the letter and crumpled it in her hand. How dare he betray her and then say it was for her own good! Did he not know that he was betraying all of Illyria, inevitably costing many lives? How could one so intelligent and experienced make such a choice?

On her trek to Scutari, Teuta had time to think long and hard about the letter, about her past. Her mind kept returning to her childhood and the times she and Demetrius had played in the fields. She tried to remember how he had acted toward her. Had she missed signs of affection? Had unrequited love led him to this point? In the end, she had no choice but to be his enemy, and that hurt her deeply. Events now set in motion could not be undone. She cried softly.

CHAPTER NINE

THE MIGHT OF THE ROMANS IS ONLY IN NUMBERS

CONSULS MARCUS PAULLUS AND Livius Salinator joined the consuls' meeting regarding what they called the Second Illyrian Conflict. Their generals were reporting in one by one that everything was ready and that they were waiting for the command from the consuls to begin their assault on Illyria.

"Has there been news about Demetrius and his soldiers?" Livius asked.

"I hear he has led his forces to Corcyra and will neither aid nor inhibit our actions," Fabius reported.

"That should be sufficient. Without his army, the Illyrians will be at a considerable disadvantage." Livius seemed satisfied, but Paullus would have none of it.

"Bring back the head of Queen Teuta, for all the crimes she has committed against Rome."

"The agreement with Demetrius is that we do not seek out or harm Queen Teuta. We are after a Kingdom, not merely the Queen. We will take from her what she prizes most. That should be ample punishment."

Paullus grunted. "I did not agree to that plan."

Fabius sighed. "Without that provision we would have the full force of Demetrius's soldiers against us and a possible defeat. I think we achieved a fair bargain."

W IND AND RAIN FOLLOWED Queen Teuta and her entourage as they rode through the dense countryside. After hours of pushing through the storm, Prince Darsej suggested they stop in the small village that lay ahead.

The inhabitants were friendly and offered hot milk and honey. Teuta and Prince Darsej dried their clothes by the fire and slept.

Teuta awoke to curious faces staring down at her. She arose and, while wrapped in a thick blanket, conversed with the elderly townspeople.

"How is life for you here in Illyria?" she asked.

The weathered and gray man dressed in skins and remnants of cloth replied, "It is as good a place as we have ever been. The Gods have blessed us with peace, and that is all we can ask."

His elderly wife smiled. "Love is all the riches we need, although a good stewing rabbit comes in second." Her eyes twinkled, and she hugged her husband.

"Thank you for your hospitality." Queen Teuta gave them some coins and a hunting bow. The couple tried to refuse the gifts, but Teuta would not have it.

This is what she and her men were fighting for—these common people and their lives of peace and love. It was the duty of the Queen and every soldier that fought on the field of battle to maintain their lives. She suddenly became anxious, wanting to turn back and join the fight.

Prince Darsej saw her dismay. "What is it, my Queen?"

"For the first time in my life, I feel a strange emptiness, a futility that I cannot shake. The memories of my King and all that has transpired no longer lift me beyond the darkness."

"Do not fear, Your Majesty. Everything will be alright. The Gods will see to it." The Prince looked into her eyes and saw the worry, the fear.

Finally the rain stopped and Queen Teuta and her entourage could see the beautiful mountains of Scutari. As they rode past the vast lake and into the city, Teuta started to breathe deeply and feel a sense of peace. She asked herself if she could rule from this place. If, hidden among these hills, she would be able to continue her duties as Queen.

ARION, GENTIUS, AND ALL the generals and advisors did not sleep. Not knowing when the Roman ships and army would arrive, they spent the time reinforcing barricades and stockpiling arrows and weapons. Teuta's pirates were on the first ships, anxious and ready for the fight. Arion and Gentius were aboard two of the Liburnia warships. Rron was sent to the Castle and told to stay away from the confrontation.

Women cooked, bringing hot meals to the soldiers. This went on for couple of days and nights until the sun rose on the third day and the glint of sails could be seen. The cry went out, "Ships ahoy, ships ahoy!" Everyone scrambled for their positions, uttering scarcely a word.

As the ships drew near, Arion and Gentius gasped. The sheer number of Roman ships darkening the sea rendered it nearly invisible. There seemed to be thousands of the vessels.

"May the Gods help us," Gentius said under his breath.

Arion had won many wars with King Agron against the Greeks and Romans, but this, what he saw in front of him, would be a hard victory at best. Still, he was ready to fight until his last breath.

Rron stood on Queen Teuta's balcony staring out across the vast fleet of warships. The sight took his breath away; he had never seen so many ships before. He suddenly realized how alone he was and that brave as he was on the training grounds, the reality of actual war sent a cold shiver over him, causing his insides to churn. He instinctively bent over the balcony and let loose the contents of his stomach. He knew that now was not the time to think of himself; he had to find Dorotea, to tell her to escape to Rhizon and make her way to Epidamnus.

Rron found her in the kitchen trying to make herself busy. She did not like the idea of leaving Rron again but eventually agreed to go to Rhizon. Donning his battle clothes, Rron helped Dorotea to her horse.

"I will be along shortly," he told her. "There are some things I need to do first." He let go of the horse's reins, and she was off.

ARION ORDERED THE SHIPS to approach the Romans head on. Gentius gave the command to ready arrows to fire from three ships, making the barrage continuous and hopefully overpowering the enemy. The ships were then directed to split into two groups and head toward the enemy's flanks. Arion hoped this would divide the Roman fleet and give the Illyrian reserves time to back up the assault.

Arrows rained down on the Romans, causing a momentary pause in their attack. But then the Romans fired back with their own, much thicker cloud of deadly projectiles.

The Illyrian ships successfully divided some of the Romans from their massive assault, but there were just too many of the enemy vessels. Arion's Liburnia plowed ahead, ramming as many ships as it could, cutting deep into the center of the Roman fleet. For a moment, the Romans seemed confused and distracted by the large ship, which gave Arion an opportunity to strike and retreat. Smaller Illyrian vessels sacrificed themselves to clear the way for Arion's Liburnia, which finally emerged on the east side of the battle with dead sailors and burning at the bow.

Fighting lasted two days and nights. Though the Illyrians fought like never before, their efforts could not overpower the sheer number of Romans. They finally broke through to the city from landside and, following orders from the consul, destroyed everything in their path.

Approaching from all sides and without the help of Demetrius's men, the Romans attacked Pharos and Sucuraj. All Arion and Gentius could do was use their ships to rescue the generals and evade capture. Taking advantage of a lull in the fighting, they met to discuss what needed to be done next. They were both exhausted and covered in blood.

"You have to stay alive and go to Queen Teuta," Arion implored. "There is no hope in saving these cities. They are lost. If you have a chance to visit Queen Apollonia, tell her I love her and that she was the last person on my mind before death."

"What kind of soldier would I be if I ran from battle? It is my duty to stay and fight alongside you until both our souls are taken by the Gods." Gentius was firm.

"It is also your duty to obey orders. And I order you to go to Queen Teuta, to be Illyria's first line of defense." Arion held Gentius' shoulders and looked into his eyes. "Go."

Gentius hesitated and the battle grew nearer. Feeling like a deserter in his very heart, Gentius jumped from the ship and swam through the bloody waters to shore.

Arion fought on, distracting as many ships as possible while the Illyrians fled. He was finally captured, defiant until the end. Tortured mercilessly, he withstood the pain and the horror. The only thing he whispered was Queen Apollonia's name. She, indeed, was the last person on his mind before he died.

WITH THE BATTLE WON, the Romans had their victory over Illyria. Yet the victory seemed hollow without the capture of Queen Teuta. She still remained at large. She still remained a threat.

CHAPTER TEN

THE WARRIOR QUEEN: THIS IS JUST THE BEGINNING

QUEEN TEUTA COULD NOT sleep or eat for five days. She only drank water.

"You have to eat some food," Dora pleaded. "You can do no one any good if you are dead."

But Teuta continued her fast until, finally, soldiers approached the stronghold. As they came nearer, she could see the glint of the sun off the swords, one of which shone red.

Gentius and the rest of the Illyrian soldiers were in bad shape, covered in dried blood—both theirs and the Romans'. Teuta ordered servants to care for the men, allowing them to recover before asking for news. It was clear, however, that what they had to say was not good.

"We held them for two days. Their numbers were overwhelming. We lost Pharos, Sucuraj, and many other territories. They burned and destroyed everything, killing even women and children. You must know that every man fought bravely until their last breath. Your pirates were fierce and shouting your name. Arion ordered me to leave the battle and come to you; otherwise, I too would be lying among the dead." Gentius tried to catch his breath.

Queen Teuta looked at him, tears forming in her eyes for all those who gave their lives for Illyria, for her, all those who had suffered and had yet to suffer.

Prince Darsej was devastated—his home gone and likely most of the people he knew and loved. Queen Teuta tried to console him. "When the pain is too big, words simply cannot measure it. I know your pain, but we will rebuild, and though we cannot bring back lives that are lost, we can tend to the living as best we can."

The Prince thanked her and retreated to his quarters. Teuta escaped to the terrace and gazed out over the beautiful countryside. The lake lay glass-still, the birds sang. But it was not enough to keep the pain from her heart.

Dora had brought King Agron's pillow along with Teuta's other things. Teuta retrieved them and hugged the pillow close to her chest. She deeply inhaled Agron's fading scent and felt his hug, his kiss. The candles surrounding her bed waned slowly. A few faint voices whispered in the distance. After a time, Teuta drifted off to sleep.

Q UEEN TEUTA ROSE OUT of bed and put on her leather war dress. A dim light was just rising behind the trees. As everyone else slept, she opened the door to the outside.

A guard approached. "My Queen, is everything alright?"

"Yes, I just need to take a walk, no need to follow me. I will be back soon."

Teuta walked aimlessly out into the countryside. She climbed the first mountain, reaching the summit a few hours later. As she stood at the pinnacle, the breeze blew her night-black hair. Tears rolled down her cheeks, but they weren't tears of sorrow. They were cleansing tears, and she smiled, recalling King Agron's words.

"Tears are simply raindrops from the storm inside us. They flow silently through the soul and cleanse the heart: they are words the heart can't say."

She spoke to him on the mountain and knew in her heart he could hear her. "I am sorry I couldn't protect Illyria. But I give my word that I will take it back. I will keep my Besa. We will be victorious once again.

D EMETRIUS RECEIVED WORD OF the Roman victory and, at the same time, that Teuta could not be found. Relieved, he knew she had escaped. He had also been told of Arion's death and the demise of many men that he had fought alongside over the years. This bothered him greatly, yet he had to remember that Illyria was saved and that he would have the authority to rebuild.

There was no doubt in Demetrius's mind that Teuta would forever be lost to him, but the sacrifice was the Gods' will. It would take a few months before he could return to Epidamnus. Once there, and having assumed the position of Regent, he would have to confront Rron and let him know what would be expected of him. Bersant would be there to help with the transition although he did not trust the man; Demetrius was fully aware that Bersant had been the intermediary between the Romans and himself, and he also knew that he had helped betray Teuta not for the love of country but out of love for influence and power. Demetrius knew he could use that to his advantage.

NORIK WAS BUSY. A vast number of Illyrians had retreated to Epidamnus, and he had to ensure that order was maintained and that Apollonia was safe. The generals who survived the Roman onslaught and what was left of the military set to work reinforcing the cities' defenses for the inevitable Roman attack. As Norik made his rounds, he listened. Hearing all sorts of stories from every side, it was hard for him to believe any of them, except the fact that Demetrius had turned against Teuta and that his alliance with the Romans had made him Rron's surrogate ruler, just as Teuta had been. So it was a surprise when, a month after the battle, Queen Teuta returned to the city where her journey with King Agron had begun. Waiting for her were Gentius, Rron, Scerdilaidas, and all those who had fought and bled for her.

The mighty, beautiful Queen stood on the hill overlooking the expanse below, the sloping fields that gave way to coastal rocks and the city of Epidamnus. She knew it was not wise for her to be there, but she had missed so much already, not having been there for her soldiers as they fought and died at the hands of the Romans. Not having been there to protect her people.

Queen Teuta held her sword out toward the horizon. The wind picked up and blew her hair in front of her face. The light from the waning sun caught her blade and reflected it out along the expanse below, making the weapon visible from the ramparts of the castle. She screamed at the empty land, releasing sorrow, frustration, and anger. She was at once a giant embracing the vista before her and an ant trying to come to terms with a blade of grass. It was as if she understood the Gods yet was more baffled than ever by them.

All the Queen really knew was that it would be two months before the Romans reached the stronghold, and this time she could not fail. The battle was lost, but the war had just begun.